UNWIN HYMAN SHORT STORIES

YOU NEVER KNOW

D0543242

LANCASHIRE
WENNINGTON HALL SCHOOL
WENNINGTON, LANCASTER
EDUCATION COMMITTEE

INCLUDING
FOLLOW ON
ACTIVITIES

EDITED BY GEOFF BARTON
AND DAVID BENNETT

Unwin Hyman English Series

Series editor: Roy Blatchford
Advisers: Jane Leggett and Gervase Phinn

Unwin Hyman Short Stories
Openings   edited by Roy Blatchford
Round Two   edited by Roy Blatchford
School's OK   edited by Josie Karavasil and Roy Blatchford
Stepping Out   edited by Jane Leggett
That'll Be The day   edited by Roy Blatchford
Sweet and Sour   edited by Gervase Phinn
It's Now or Never   edited by Jane Leggett and Roy Blatchford
Pigs is Pigs   edited by Trevor Millum
Dreams and Resolutions   edited by Roy Blatchford
Shorties   edited by Roy Blatchford
First Class   edited by Michael Bennett
Snakes and Ladders   edited by Hamish Robertson
Crying for Happiness   edited by Jane Leggett
Funnybones   edited by Trevor Millum
You Never Know   edited by Geoff Barton and David Bennett

Unwin Hyman Collections
Free As I know   edited by Beverley Naidoo
Solid Ground   edited by Jane Leggett and Sue Libovitch
In our Image   edited by Andrew Goodwyn
Northern Lights   edited by Leslie Wheeler

Unwin Hyman Plays
Stage Write   edited by Gervase Phinn
Right on Cue   edited by Gervase Phinn
Scriptz   edited by Ian Lumsden

ISBN 0 00 322279 9

Published in 1992 by
CollinsEducational
an imprint of HarperCollins*Publishers*
77–85 Fulham Palace Road
Hammersmith, London W6 8JB

Typeset by Northern Phototypesetting Co Ltd., Bolton
Printed in Great Britain by Billing & Sons Ltd., Worcester
Series cover design by Iain Lanyon. Cover illustration by Mark Haddon.
Illustrations by Terry McKenna (pp. 13, 21, 78, 118) and Mark Haddon
(pp. 34, 52, 65, 84, 103).

CONTENTS

Introduction

In compiling this collection of stories, we were advised by a group of thirteen 14–15 year olds at Garforth Comprehensive School, near Leeds. They in fact made many of the editorial decisions. Here they describe the process of selecting stories and designing the front cover:

We created this book for 14–16 year olds who do not usually enjoy reading!

We chose the stories by reading them aloud a number of times, giving our views, saying what we liked or disliked about the ideas, storyline and characters. Before we decided whether a story should be included in the final book, we usually read it again on our own or in pairs. Sometimes, if there was a story which we liked but which needed some changes, we would write to the author and ask if he or she would alter some parts. Many of the stories in the book were rewritten for us by the authors – thanks!

As well as choosing the stories for the book, we had to select the cover design. We started by looking at the covers of all the other books in the series. We also had some samples of work done by different illustrators. We particularly liked the artwork of Mark Haddon – he draws very funny cartoons of people and uses bright colours. We sent him a brief which asked for different characters from the stories to be mixed up together. It was to look funny, but not babyish.

Mark Haddon sent us a first draft of his ideas, which we liked. We made a few suggestions – for example, the cat did not really look too much like a cat. Then he went ahead and created the front cover in full colour. We hope it does not look too much like an ordinary school book!

We found the most difficult part was choosing a title for the book. Some of the ideas we had were: 'Other World', 'Tale Enders', 'Spotlights', 'Fingerprints', 'Live Wires' and 'Maybe Tomorrow'. We finally decided to take the title from the shortest story in the book.

That is how we put the book together. So read and enjoy it. We did!

Philip Bailie, Adrian Garbutt, Donna Hitchen, Daniel Kelly,
Donna Quayle, Sarah Munro, Antony Oxley, Nicola Poppleton,
Peter Shooter, Darren Smith, Paul Staniforth, Emma Theaker,
Ryan Whitaker.

BEVERLEY NAIDOO
Whose Hair is it Anyway?

I have always wanted to try my hand at hairdressing – for real, I mean. When I was seven I got Mum to give me one of those doll's heads from Santa – you know the sort, with long nylon hair, cute little spiky curlers and a pink plastic hairdryer. (Of course I had found out about Santa by then but I didn't let on 'cause Mum used to give me a present from her and Dad as well.) I would spend hours fiddling with Sophie's hair I called her Sophie because I had overheard Mum talking about how 'sophisticated' children were nowadays and I thought it sounded really grown-up. Anyway all my other dolls had names, so why shouldn't Sophie? Just because she only had a head, it didn't mean she hadn't got feelings, did it?

But playing with Sophie's hair wasn't like doing the real thing. I gradually got bored with pretending I was 'Julie' or 'Rachel' – a top stylist at Watford's top salon – and Sophie was left on my dressing table, for months on end, her stare fixed on me through perfectly round blue eyes. Her hair gathered dust like everything else in my room between one 'Operation Clean-Up' and the next.

Much more fun than playing with Sophie, however, was getting my hands onto proper hair. My best time was when we were going to Ireland. I was only about six at the time and I sat cramped in the back seat with Mum and my brother, while our friends drove us. Maureen has really long hair, which she let hang over her seat just in front of me. It was the same reddish colour as Sophie's but more natural – and she let me brush it, all the way to Ireland! Well, nearly all the way before we got on the boat. Every now and again she would ask for a little rest and I would sit untangling the fine strands of hair from the brush until she was ready to let me start again.

Sometimes I also used to get a chance to try out plaits and bits and pieces of styles on some of my friends with long hair

1

during story-time at school. That was when we were a lot younger and we used to sit on a mat in the story corner. The best place to be was at the far side of the teacher, so she could only really see you if she had sideways eyes like a squirrel, or if she turned her head. I'm saying 'she' because all my teachers in the infants and lower juniors were women. It's funny, but the only two men teachers always seemed to stick with the older children. Maybe they thought we needed people like mummies when we were little more than people like daddies. Mind you when my mum gets at me, I can tell you I need my dad!

I could also have done with my dad for protection the day my teacher caught me making Sarah turn her head so I could plait the last strands above her left ear. Somehow I had got carried away after making six plaits around the back of her head, neatly finished off with blue elastic bands (brought from home) and matching beads (borrowed from the bead-tin in the maths tray). It was a brilliant story, too, that she interrupted, just to tell me off, all about a girl called Rapunzel.

But on the whole, fiddling with other people's hair doesn't cause any major problems. It's like knitting – you can unpick and start again. Perhaps that has been its fascination for me, the idea of endless possibility. Now cutting . . . that's another matter. It's not that hair won't regrow, but at the point when you actually snip the scissors together and see a loop of hair tumble off, there's something final about it. I cried after my first and only attempt at giving Sophie a new look. I guessed it was going to go wrong after I had taken the first small snip with Mum's nail scissors. But I could see I had to go on and although I didn't take off very much, by the time I had finished, she was never again to be the perfect model for a salon photograph.

I am still puzzled about why on earth I tried cutting my own hair. It was four years ago, when I was nine. Perhaps I was suffering from not being able to play with my friends' hair so much. We no longer had stories on a mat in the corner and there just weren't so many opportunities. After our class went swimming I could offer to help a friend with long hair, but dealing with tangled damp hair isn't quite the same, especially with Mr Masters yelling at you to hurry up. The atmosphere wasn't the same any more. I think I must have been in a bad or mad mood that day, because I loved my thick dark hair being so long and being able to do different things with it. In fact, when Mum used to get irritated because I was spending hours sorting out my hair instead of getting ready for school, she would say, 'We really should get your hair cut!'

But I would protest loudly, 'No, you won't! It's *my* hair!'

All I can remember when I went mad with the scissors on my own hair, was a sense of power. Funny to have power over your own hair and yourself! It was long enough for me to hold thick batches of it out sideways and watch it in the mirror as I tried to add a professional look to my scissor movement. It fell in thick chunks. I studied the new me. Who was that person in the mirror?

Mum's first reaction was, 'Oh my God! What have you done?'

Dad, on the other hand, immediately found the whole affair a joke.

'What are you complaining about?' he said to Mum. 'You wanted her to have it short! It's only a bit wonky!'

He must have seen the tears welling up in my eyes. I obviously wasn't in control that day after all. He put his arm around me.

'Don't worry, my darling! It'll grow again!'

A real philosopher is my dad.

So what possessed me to offer to cut Gemma's hair yesterday? I can't say it was a spur of the moment decision. Kathy, Lizzie, Gemma and I have been into 'hair talk' for ages at school. It's not that we don't chat about lots of other things, of course we do. But it's something we've got in common – we've all got long hair. At least we had it in common – until yesterday.

The idea must have started growing in my mind ever since Gemma began saying she wanted to have her hair cut, but her mum said no, she couldn't afford to take her to the hairdressers. I felt really sorry for her. But I don't think I knew exactly what was growing in my mind – that little speck of an idea getting bigger and stronger until one day, Pow!

'Why don't we all meet up at my house on Sunday and we can do each other's hair? I can cut yours for you, Gemma, if you like.'

Everyone thought it was a terrific plan. I only had to persuade Mum to let me have my friends round, and that wasn't difficult. I promised we wouldn't make any noise to disturb her typing and she said it would be fine as long as she didn't have to go out for a meeting. By Saturday she confirmed it was OK, so I got Dad to take me to the shops to buy some drink and crisps for the occasion. I didn't say anything to Mum about the hair session. I'm not sure why. Maybe I just didn't think it was anything to do with her . . . you know the way you think some things are just between you and your friends.

We had a great time – choice music from my albums, food, drink, Kathy's new shampoo, Gemma's pink ringlet curling sticks (for me to try out) and Mum's razor-sharp hair scissors. We shut the door although Mum and Dad were very considerate, getting on with their own things and letting us get on with enjoying ourselves.

Gemma, seated in front of the dressing table mirror, said she wanted about four inches off, so I set to work. Her hair is very curly so it certainly wasn't a matter of just cutting straight. She was smiling and giggling and in fact we were all pretty happy. Only when I was about half way through my creation, did Gemma introduce a slightly worrying note.

'Oh dear! What if my mum is cross? Perhaps she really doesn't want me to have my hair cut.'

I don't think my mum even noticed that Gemma's hair had been shortened when she came upstairs to tell Gemma her Dad was waiting outside. She noticed our hair was wet though.

'Goodness! Have you all been washing your hair?'

'Yes, it's rather a weird thing to do when you go visiting, isn't it!' laughed Kathy, standing in front of the bedroom door so Mum wouldn't come in.

I was very pleased with the ringlet effect from Gemma's curlers, that is, until my brother called me Medusa and mentioned snakes. Don't brothers somehow have a knack of ruining things? That was the one picture in my book of legends that really gave me nightmares – all those twisted snakes crawling out of the monster-woman's head. But on the whole, it had been a good day. Gemma and the others had liked the final result of my handiwork, and I might even have tried out the ringlet curlers overnight for extra effect, if it hadn't been for the Medusa comment. Drifting off into a pleasurable semi-dream in bed, recreating highlights of the day, I was only vaguely aware of the telephone ringing and Mum answering it.

Mum called me into her room first thing this morning.

'Do you know who rang last night?'

It had been Gemma's dad. He said that his wife was too furious to speak, so he was ringing for her. My mum was totally taken by surprise because he asked if she knew what we had been up to. Mum had to say no and so he had told her. According to what he said, Gemma is not going to be allowed out to friends, and her mum thinks the hair so much a mess that she will have to take her to a hairdresser after all.

'But Mum,' I began to sob, 'that's why I offered to cut it . . . because her mum had said she couldn't afford it.'

I didn't add any excuses to do with how much I love handling hair. I could see Mum was angry, too.

'Didn't you realise what could happen? Do you really think Gemma's mother will ever let her come to visit you again?'

It is as if life has come tumbling down on me . . . just like the flock of Gemma's golden hair which landed in the bin. Mum has seen it now. I feel so sorry for Gemma, and so sorry for myself that I can't stop crying. I have just written a letter to Gemma's parents saying it was all my fault and I am sending them a cheque from my mum to pay for the hairdresser. I'm going to pay Mum back from my pocket money.

I shall have to stop crying because I have to go to school. I only hope Gemma isn't mad at me now. I know I shouldn't have done it, because look at the trouble we are in. But, you know, there is still one question which keeps going round and round in my mind. I can't get rid of it. Whose hair is it anyway?

PS   You'll never guess what happened at school today. Lots of people came up to me and said, 'Rukshana! You're a brilliant haircutter!'

In fact three girls are going home to ask their mums if I can cut their hair!

However, perhaps they had better first ask their dads. Gemma told me that her mum actually quite liked what I had done, but it was her dad who had hit the roof!

Does *that* answer my question?

ALAN GARNER

The Salmon Cariad

There was a Welsh youth went fishing on a river one moonlight night. He sat in his coracle, as they call it, and he had his paddle tucked under his arm, and he was holding on to his rod and the knocker for killing the fish, all at the same time, when a great salmon jumped up and took the fly.

The coracle waltzed round, bobbing and spinning, and what with trying to paddle and trying to play the line, it was lob's chance whether the youth would catch the salmon or the salmon would catch him.

Anyway, at the finish, he got it over the side and into the coracle. It was a big salmon; it was that. It lay there, flapping its tail, and gasping; and he picked up the knocker to hit it on the head with. But all of a sudden it twisted and reared up against his leg, and it said, 'Be my cariad.'

Well, you can imagine. There he was, in the middle of the river, with the knocker lifted in his hand, and the salmon said, 'Be my Cariad.' Cariad is what you call a body in Wales when you're sweet on them; and there was the fish, talking to him, and giving him cariad!

But, 'No,' says the youth. 'I'm going to knock you on the head.' (You see he kept his wits about him.)

And the salmon says back at him, 'Be my cariad; and I shall be your cariad.'

'No,' says he. 'I'm going to knock you on the head.' And he pulled back his arm to biff the salmon a good un – when that salmon gave another twist of its tail and bumped against him and fetched him down, and he landed in a heap on top of the salmon and skrawked his face on its scales. But it wasn't rightly scales any more. No. It was skin. Cold wet skin. And he found himself held tight; and he looked; and he saw there was no salmon, but a woman, with her arms fast around him and her face close against his.

7

'Be my cariad,' she says.

'No, I will not!' says the youth. 'I'll knock you on the head!'

'Then I'll drown you,' she says. And she held on to him, and she hutched and thrutched, and tipped the both of them in the water.

She took him deep under, what's more, and then she brought him up for air.

'Be my cariad,' she says.

'No, I'll not!' he says.

'Down you go,' she says. And down he went!

Up again she fetched him, and he was in a poor way by now.

'Be my cariad,' she says.

'No,' he says.

Down they went again, into the weeds and such. Up they come.

'Be my cariad,' she says, and this time he thinks he might as good wed a fish as be going up and down in the river all night; so he says, 'All right,' he says. 'I'll be your cariad.'

'Good lad,' she says; and she held him up out of the water and swum him to the bank.

He grabbed and pulled himself up on the grass; but the coracle and all his gear, they were taken by the water and washed away. And he was left with this woman; well, a girl, more like, nearer his age, white as a salmon, and not a stitch on her.

She wasn't feeling too good herself, now, for she'd been hooked as a fish, and that hook was still in her, through her lip; and the rod was in the coracle yonder and being carried off by the river; so she wasn't very comfortable. She was trying to get the hook out, but not having much success.

'Here,' says the youth, for he couldn't help but pity her, 'give over wriggling. I'll get the hook out.'

So he did his best; but the hook was fast in.

'It's no use,' he says. 'It'll have to be my little knife. I must cut you.'

'Ay,' she says. 'Cut me.'

So he took his knife, and he cut the hook out; and she never budged. But as soon as that hook was free, she lifted her face to his, and she kissed him hard, right on the mouth, so that he couldn't help getting her blood on him, and tasting it, too.

'And now you've taken my blood on you,' she says, 'you must love me for ever.'

And would you credit it, but he did love her! From that moment, he was full of love; and she loved him; and he took her home and lived with her a long and lucky life, and they had a heap of children.

Now there's not a great lot more to tell. There was one thing about them, though, that was a bit queer. Every single child that they had was born with a little white scar, or what seemed like one, on the top lip, a bit to the left. I knew one of their lads. He used to come out of Wales driving cattle to market, and it was him who told me the tale; and I've seen his scar.

RICHARD BENNETT

Eddy's Great Climb

My name is Eddy Wilson. I'm in the fifth year. The teachers at school find me difficult. I play them up because I can't understand what they are going on about.

Mrs Williams is my Support Teacher. She's the only teacher who bothers to help me. You see, I find it very difficult to read. I even find it difficult to write. Without Mrs Williams I would die.

The rest of the teachers don't really care about me. So I don't go to their lessons. I go to the betting shop instead. I don't get shown up there because I know what I'm doing.

I'm now in my fifth year at school. Anybody who is thick like me gets to spend a lot of time on the computer. It gets on my nerves, pressing all those stupid buttons just to write a sentence. Mrs Williams is so patient with me. She never loses her temper. I feel like smashing the stupid screen sometimes. But she helps me a lot. The only reason I'm in school is because of her.

The best time I've ever had at this rotten school was last summer. We had something called 'Trips Week'. That means we go away for a week and some of the teachers come with us. It's like going away on holiday with the school. Instead of lying on the beach in the sun, I got to do loads of different things.

I chose a trip to the Joe Brown Outdoor Centre, Bangor, North Wales. I had a whole week canoeing and climbing. I didn't have to read or write much either. I want to tell you about my trip to the Joe Brown Outdoor Centre because it changed me. It changed me so much.

I could not believe I was sitting on the coach and we were on our way. I sat with John Page who is my best mate. I'd already eaten my dinner. It was ten o'clock in the morning. We'd only started out at nine o'clock! I was starving so I ate half of John Page's dinner and everybody else's left-overs.

We arrived at the Joe Brown Outdoor Centre just in time for a late tea. The centre was really a big house with loads of small rooms. I think it was an old hotel which overlooked the sea.

We were given our tea and shown to our rooms. I ended up on the top bunk with John Page sleeping below me. There were six other lads in the room. The view from the room was brilliant. I'd only ever seen the sea once before.

We were awake at seven o'clock in the morning. That morning some of us went canoeing. I was gob-struck when I found out that Pauline Wood was in my group. That made me really scared. I was so scared because I fancied her like mad. If she ever spoke to me I would die on the spot. If ever she looked at me I thought it was my lucky day. She was so good looking it was untrue.

Chris Day was also in my group. I remember, last year, having a scrap with him. It was over Pauline Wood. I nearly broke his head in two when he said I'd got no chance of going out with her. He was right, of course but I didn't like the way he said it. The only way I could show my anger was to batter him and batter him good. I have a hell of a temper when I get going. One day it's going to get me into big trouble.

I'd never go out with Pauline Wood. Nobody wants to go out with a thick bastard like Eddy Wilson.

Sitting in my canoe, I kept very quiet. I was scared I'd do something wrong and Pauline Wood would notice. We learnt about canoeing on a small lake. We had to paddle our canoes in a straight line. Pauline Wood was perfect at canoeing. I was all over the place. I felt a right wally. Going in a straight line was difficult, but even more difficult was going upside down in the water. Everybody in the group had to stay in their canoe and go upside down under water, then try to get out of the canoe. Its called Capsize Drill.

One by one everyone in the group had to have a go at Capsize Drill. I couldn't believe it when Pauline Wood wanted to go first. She did it without any problems. Deep breath, over, under, push, roll and out. She glided out of the canoe. As her face broke the surface of the water, she smiled with relief. Her blonde hair smoothed behind her shoulders. Lovely.

Mrs Williams went next. At nearly 50 years old she looked like an old hand. Deep breath, over, under, push, roll and out. She splashed her way out of the canoe. We all clapped in wonder. I clapped so hard I lost my balance and my canoe slowly twisted over in the water with me in it! I had no time to think about deep breath, over, under, push, roll and out. There was nothing I could do but panic. I thought about getting my legs out of the canoe. They would not move and I was gasping for air.

Suddenly, somehow, I was safe. I popped up onto the surface of the lake. The rest of the group laughed and clapped. I felt like a right dummy. Pauline Wood was laughing, too. I laughed, but inside I was bricking myself. Inside I thought, 'What am I doing here? Am I enjoying this?' The answer was 'Yes'.

The next day, Wednesday, we went on a sea trip. We went in our canoes. It was great. We saw seals, jelly fish, sea birds and . . . a dead body. It was washed up on the shore, stiff, white and half eaten. John Page was the first to see it. He shouted at the top of his voice 'There's a dead body over here!' We all went to look. It was only a dead fish. It was John Page's idea of a joke.

That night we camped out on an island. We were miles from anywhere and anyone. The night was clear. I was sharing a tent with John Page. John Page was my best mate. He was my best mate because he did stupid things. He had somehow managed to hide some cans of beer in the bottom of his sleeping bag. He wasn't supposed to have them.

Don't ask me why. It seemed a good idea at the time. It was against the rules, so we did it . . .

We drank the lot between us. By one o'clock in the morning we were both flat out. We were legless. Thanks to the beer, the world seemed a great place to be.

John Page was thick, as well as stupid. The next morning, Mrs Williams woke us up to find our tent full of empty cans. We were smelling of beer. We were guilty. John Page had forgotten to put the empty cans at the bottom of his sleeping

bag. We were oh, so guilty.

The teachers had told us before the trip had started that anybody caught drinking alcohol would be sent home.

I could have killed John Page for making me do something so stupid. Worst of all, I found out he'd nicked the beer from the corner shop near to the Joe Brown Outdoor Centre. We were in trouble. We were going home. I was going to batter John Page.

I had never seen Mrs Williams so angry. She threw a wobbler at me and John Page. Her red face and loud voice said it all. I had let her down. I was as sick as a parrot. I admit I was close to tears.

My dad was out of work. He'd spent most of his money on booze or on the horses. The reason I was on this trip was because he'd put £5 on a horse that came in at 8 to 1. He was going to kill me. Oh God. Help!

The rest of the group helped John Page and me pack away our tent. We put the empty cans in a plastic bag. Pauline Wood picked up a beer can and read out loud the name on the label, 'Hall's Lager Beer, Alcohol Free'.

Alcohol free! John Page had pinched the wrong beer, because he couldn't read the label! We thought we were legless and we weren't! Mrs Williams picked up a can and she read the label too: 'Hall's Lager Beer, Alcohol Free'.

We were saved! Thank God John Page couldn't read. I could have kissed Pauline Wood but I didn't. I was dancing on the spot. Mrs Williams agreed that we could stay. But John Page had to go back to the Corner Shop and pay for the 'Hall's Lager Beer, Alcohol Free'.

John Page said he felt a right prat giving the bloke at the shop his empty cans back. And then paying for them!

We were so lucky!

For the last two days of the trip we went climbing on Rocky Sea Cliffs. The 90 foot cliffs were about the same height as a Tesco's Superstore. This one cliff was called 'Sea Face'. It dropped straight down into the sea. A big wall, 90 feet high with the sea bashing against the base of the rock. It was a scary place. But we were going to climb up it.

The coppers at home had always said I was a good climber.

They only ever caught me once. That was after the drain pipe up the outside of the school sports hall came away from the wall. I told you it was a rotten school. I twisted my ankle. The coppers nearly twisted my head off when they caught me!

At Sea Face the whole group sat on a bit of a rock waiting to climb. The angry sea sprayed us through the sunshine. I could see that a lot of the group were nervous. Chris Bates was biting his nails. Mrs Williams was very quiet.

One by one, the group climbed up 'Sea Face'. I was left waiting at the bottom with Mrs Williams. The sea splashed against the rocks. Mrs Williams was scared. I have never seen anybody shake so much. The long wait for the rope to come down was making things worse . . . Mrs Williams began to cry. I was gob-struck.

Mrs Williams crying because she was scared of heights? The tough, hard Mrs Williams scared? Crying? What was going on? I thought at first it was a joke. But it wasn't, it was for real. Mrs Williams could not move.

For me, in that one moment, the whole world seemed to click into place. I now understood things a lot more. It wasn't just me who had a problem. I was scared to read. Mrs Williams was scared of heights. Everybody was scared of something. Everybody has their own problems. I was scared of reading because I'd never really faced up to it. I still didn't know my 'on's from my 'no's. I didn't want to read books because it was a show-up. And here was Mrs Williams crying because I guess she'd been shown up.

I don't know why I said it, but I did. I told Mrs Williams that if she climbed up Sea Face, I, Eddy Wilson, would promise to learn to read properly. I swore on my mother's life. The promise made Mrs Williams climb.

With all her courage, Mrs Williams faced up to her problem. She took a deep breath, clipped on the safety rope and slowly began to climb Sea Face. Fifteen minutes later she reached the top. To Mrs Williams it was as if she'd just climbed Everest.

I quickly followed. I didn't even notice the climb. To be honest, I found it easy. To me, it was easy.

I was thinking of other things. I was thinking, when I got back to school I *must* learn to read well. I *must* learn to write well. I *must* face up to my problem. I knew Mrs Williams would help me even more now.

I swear that trip to the Joe Brown Outdoor Centre was the best thing that ever happened to me. It made me want to help myself. It made me face up to my problem and do something about it.

Back at school, Mrs Williams was there to help. I faced up to reading 'on's and 'no's. I felt a right wally copying out letters. I did it because it didn't matter what other people thought. I did it so that if I nicked some beer it would be real beer, because I could read the label.

Over a period of about three months, I worked my socks off. Very slowly I began to read a lot better. I even managed to fill out the stupid work experience form the teachers gave us.

I thought to myself this rotten school will never send me back to the Joe Brown Outdoor Centre. But they did. For two weeks I helped teach climbing . . . with Pauline Wood!

JUDY CORBALIS

The Wrestling Princess

Once upon a time there was a princess who was six feet tall, who liked her own way and who loved to wrestle. Every day, she would challenge the guards at her father's palace to wrestling matches and every day, she won. Then she would pick up the loser and fling him on the ground, but gently, because she had a very kind nature.

The princess had one other unusual hobby. She liked to drive forklift trucks. Because she was a princess, and her father was very rich, she had three forklift trucks of her own – a blue one, a yellow one, and a green and purple striped one, with a coronet on each side. Whenever there was a royal parade, the king would ride in front in his golden carriage, behind him would ride a company of soldiers and behind them came the princess driving her striped royal forklift truck. The king got very cross about it but the princess simply said, 'If I can't drive my forklift truck, I won't go,' and because she was such a good wrestler, the king was too scared to disagree with her.

One day, when the princess had wrestled with sixteen soldiers at once and had beaten them all, the king sent a page to tell her to come to see him in the royal tea-room.

The princess was annoyed.

'Is it urgent?' she asked the page. 'I was just greasing the axle of my blue forklift truck.'

'I think you should come, Your Highness,' said the page, respectfully. 'His Majesty was in a terrible temper. He's burnt four pieces of toast already and dropped butter all over his second-best ermine robe.'

'Oh gosh,' said the princess, 'I'd better come right away.'

So she got up, picked up her oilcan and went into the royal bathroom to wash her hands for tea. She left oil marks all over the gold taps and the page sent a message to the palace housekeeper to clean them quickly before the king saw them.

The princess went down to the tea-room and knocked loudly on the door. A herald opened it. 'The Princess Ermyntrude!' he announced.

'About time, too,' said the king. 'And where have you been?'

'Greasing the axle of the blue forklift truck,' answered the princess politely.

The king put his head in his hands and groaned.

'This can't go on,' he sighed tragically. 'When *will* you stop messing about with these dirty machines, Ermyntrude? You're nearly sixteen and you need a husband. I must have a successor.'

'I'll succeed you, father,' cried the princess cheerfully. 'I'd love to be a king.'

'You can't be a king,' said the king sadly. 'It's not allowed.'

'Why not?' asked the princess.

'I don't know,' said the king. 'I don't make the laws. Ask the judges – it's their affair. Anyway, you can't and that's that. You have to have a husband.'

He picked up his tapestry and moodily started sewing.

'Ermyntrude,' he said after a long silence, 'you won't get a husband if you don't change your ways.'

'Why ever not?' asked the princess, in surprise.

'To get a husband you must be enchantingly beautiful, dainty and weak,' said the king.

'Well, I'm not,' said Ermyntrude cheerfully. 'I'm nothing to look at, I'm six feet tall and I'm certainly not weak. Why, Father, did you hear, this morning I wrestled with sixteen guards at once and I defeated them all?'

'Ermyntrude!' said the king sternly, as he rethreaded his needle with No. 9 blue tapestry cotton. 'Ermyntrude, we are not having any more wrestling and no more forklift trucks either. If you want a husband, you will have to become delicate and frail.'

'I *don't* want a husband,' said the princess and she stamped her foot hard. The toast rack wobbled. '*You* want me to have a husband. I just want to go on wrestling and looking after my trucks and driving in parades.'

'Well, you can't,' said the king. 'And that's that. I shall lock up the forklift trucks and instruct the guards that there is to be no more wrestling and we shall have a contest to find you a husband.'

The princess was furiously angry.

'Just you wait,' she shouted rudely. 'I'll ruin your stupid old contest. How dare you lock up my forklift trucks. You're a rotten mean old pig!'

'Ermyntrude,' said the king sternly, putting down his tapestry, 'you will do as you are told.' And he got up and left the royal tea-room.

Princess Ermyntrude was very, very angry. She bent the toasting fork in half and stamped on the bread.

'Stupid, stupid, stupid,' she said crossly. And she went away to think out a plan.

The first contest to find a prince to marry the Princess Ermyntrude took place next day. The king had beamed a message by satellite to all the neighbouring countries, and helicopters with eligible princes in them were arriving in dozens at the palace heliport.

The princess watched them from the window of her room where she was sulking.

'Stupid, stupid,' she said. 'Why, not one of them even pilots his own helicopter.'

And she went on sulking.

After lunch, the king sent a messenger to announce that the princess was to dress in her best robes and come to the great hall of the palace.

She put on her golden dress and her fur cape and her small golden crown and her large golden shoes (for she had big feet) and down she went.

At the door of the throne room she stopped to give the herald time to announce her name. Then she went in.

Seated inside were seventy-two princes, all seeking her hand in marriage.

The princess looked at them all. They all looked back.

'Sit here, my dear,' said the king loudly, and under his breath, he added, 'and behave yourself!'

The princess said nothing.

19

'Good afternoon and welcome to you all,' began the king. 'We are here today to find a suitable husband for the lovely Princess Ermyntrude, my daughter. The first competition in this contest will be that of height. As you know the princess is a very tall girl. She cannot have a husband shorter than herself so you will all line up while the Lord Chamberlain measures you.'

The seventy-two princes lined up in six rows and the Lord Chamberlain took out the royal tape measure and began to measure them.

'Why can't I have a shorter husband?' whispered the princess.

'Be quiet. You just can't,' said the king.

'Forty-eight princes left in the contest, Your Majesty,' cried the Lord Chamberlain.

'Thank you,' said the king. 'I'm sorry you gentlemen had a wasted journey but you are welcome at the banquet this evening.'

And he bowed very low.

'The second competition,' said the king 'will be that of disposition. The Princess Ermyntrude has a beautiful disposition, none better, but she does have a slightly hasty temper. She cannot have a husband who cannot match her temper. So we shall have a face-pulling, insult-throwing contest. The Lord Chamberlain will carry your names one by one and you will come forward and confront the princess, pull the worst face you can manage, put on a temper display and insult her.'

'Your Majesty, is this wise? Twenty-four of the princes have retired in confusion already,' hissed the Lord Chamberlain.

'Weaklings,' murmured the princess sweetly.

The first prince stepped forward. The Princess Ermyntrude pulled a repulsive face and he burst into tears.

'Eliminated,' said the Lord Chamberlain running forward with a box of tissues. 'Next!'

The next and the next after him and the prince following *them* were all eliminated and it was not until the fifth competitor crossed his eyes, stuck out his tongue and shouted, 'Silly cry baby,' at the princess, making her so angry

that she forgot to shout back, that anyone succeeded at all.

The fifth prince inspired the next four after him but the princes after that were no match for Princess Ermyntrude until the eighteenth and nineteenth princes called her, 'Crow face' and 'Squiggle bum' and made her giggle.

By the end of the contest, there were seven princes left, all taller and more insulting than the princess.

'And now,' said the king, 'for the third and final contest. The third competition,' he continued, 'will be that of strength. As you may know, the Princess Ermyntrude is very strong. She cannot have a weaker husband so you will all line up and wrestle with her.'

'Why can't I have a weaker husband?' whispered the princess.

'Be quiet. You just can't,' said the king.

So the Lord Chamberlain lined up the seven princes and just as they were being given their instructions, the princess, who was flexing her arm muscles, glanced over at the watching crowd of commoners and noticed a short man covered in helicopter engine oil standing at the back. Because she was so tall, Princess Ermyntrude could see him clearly and, as she looked, he looked back at her and winked quite distinctly. The princess looked again. The short man winked again.

'*Helicopter* engine oil!' thought the princess. 'That's the sort of man I like.'

Just then the short man looked at her and, forming his mouth carefully, whispered silently, 'Choose the seventh. Don't beat him.'

The princess felt strangely excited. She looked again. The little man pointed discreetly to the tall, nervous looking prince at the end of the line-up. 'That one,' he mouthed.

Princess Ermyntrude didn't much like the look of the seventh prince but she did want to please the helicopter mechanic so she nodded discreetly, rolled up her golden sleeves and stepped forward to take on the first prince.

CRASH! He hit the mat with staggering force.

CRASH, CRASH, CRASH, CRASH, CRASH.

The next five princes followed. The poor seventh prince was looking paler and paler and his knees were beginning to buckle under him. The princess looked quickly at the mechanic who nodded briefly, then she moved towards the seventh prince. He seized her feebly by the arm.

'Good heavens, I could floor him with one blow,' thought the princess, but she didn't. Instead, she let herself go limp and floppy and two seconds later, for the first time in her life, she lay flat on her back on the floor.

The crowd let out a stupendous cheer. The king and the Lord Chamberlain rushed forward and seized the hands of the young prince.

The poor prince looked very pale.

'This is terrible, terrible,' he muttered desperately.

'Nonsense,' cried the king. 'I award you the hand of the princess and half my kingdom.'

'But Sire . . .' stammered the prince. 'I can't.'

'Can't!' shouted the king. 'What do you mean *can't*. You can and you will or I'll have you beheaded!'

There was a scuffle in the crowd and the helicopter mechanic darted forward and bent low at the king's feet.

'Majesty,' he murmured reverently, 'Majesty. I am the prince's helicopter pilot, mechanic and aide. Prince Florizel is overcome with shock and gratitude. Is that not so, Sire?'' he asked, turning to the prince.

'Um, yes, yes, that's right,' said the prince nervously.

The mechanic smiled.

'Prince Florizel, of course, must have the blessing of *his* father, the King of Buzzaramia, whose kingdom adjoins your own, before the ceremony can take place. Is that not so, Sire?'

'Definitely,' said the prince.

'Quite, quite,' said the king, 'I favour these old customs myself. The princess will fly there tomorrow to meet him, in her own royal helicopter.'

'And I shall pilot myself,' said the princess.

'We shan't go into *that* now,' said the king. 'Here, you may kiss the princess.'

With a small sigh, the prince fainted dead away.

'Shocked,' said the pilot hastily. 'Clearly shocked, Your Majesty. It's not every day he wins the hand of such a beautiful, charming and talented young lady.'

And he looked deep into the princess's eyes.

The prince was carried out to his helicopter and flown off by his pilot, with instructions that the Princess Ermyntrude would fly in the following day.

The rest of the contestants and the princess had a large and elegant banquet with a six-metre chocolate cake in the shape of a heart and litres of ice-cream.

'Who made that heart?' asked Ermyntrude.

'I ordered it from Cook,' said the king.

'Well, *I* think it's soppy. A heart!' said the princess in disgust.

Next morning she was up early and, dressed in her frog-green flying suit and bright red aviator goggles, she slipped out to her helicopter before the king was up, climbed in and was just warming up the engine when the Lord Chamberlain came rushing out into the garden.

'Stop, stop,' he cried waving his arms wildly. 'Stop. His Majesty, your father, is coming too.'

The Princess Ermyntrude turned off the master switch and leaned out of the window.

'Well, he'd better hurry and I'm piloting,' she said carelessly. 'I'll wait three minutes and I'm going if he hasn't come by then.'

The Lord Chamberlain rushed into the palace and returned with the king hastily pulling his ermine robe over his nightshirt and replacing his nightcap with a crown.

'You're a dreadful girl, Ermyntrude,' he said sadly. 'Here I am with a hangover from the chocolate cake and you insist on being selfish.'

'I'm *not* selfish,' said Ermyntrude. 'I'm by far the best pilot in the palace and it's your own fault you've got a hangover if you will encourage Cook to put rum in the chocolate cake. Anyway, all this was your idea. I'm not marrying that silly prince. I'm flying over to tell him so.'

'Ermyntrude,' cried the king, scandalized. 'How can you do such a thing? I'll be ruined. He won the contest. And besides, you've got to marry someone.'

'I haven't and I won't,' said the princess firmly and she set the rotor blades in action.

Within an hour, they were flying into the next kingdom and soon they could see the palace shining golden on the highest hilltop.

'Over there,' said the king mournfully. 'Please change your mind, Ermyntrude.'

'Never,' said the princess positively. 'Never, never, never, never, never.'

Below them they could see the landing pad with ostrich feathers and fairy-lights along the strip.

Princess Ermyntrude settled the helicopter gently on the ground, waited for the blades to stop turning and got out.

The prince's mechanic was standing on the tarmac. 'A perfect landing,' he cried admiringly.

The Princess Ermyntrude smiled. Just then, an older man in ermine trimmed pyjamas came running across the grass.

'Florizel, Florizel, what is all this?' he cried.

The mechanic picked up an oilcan from beside his feet.

'Put that down, you ninny,' cried the man in ermine pyjamas. 'Don't you know this is a royal princess?'

'You're being ridiculous, Father,' said the mechanic. 'Of course I know she's a princess. I'm going to marry her.'

'*You* are?' cried Princess Ermyntrude's father. 'My daughter's not marrying you. She's marrying your prince.'

'I am marrying him,' said the Princess Ermyntrude.

'She certainly is,' said the mechanic. 'And in case you're wondering, I *am* Prince Florizel. The other one was an imposter.'

'But how?' asked the princess.

'Well,' said Prince Florizel, 'it was all my father's idea that I should go so I persuaded my mechanic to change places with me. I thought my father would never find out. Then, when I saw the Princess Ermyntrude, I fell instantly in love with her. She had axle grease on her neck and she was so big and strong. Then I realized it was lucky I'd changed places or you'd have eliminated me on height.'

'That's right. You're too short,' said the king.

'He's not,' said the princess.

'No, I'm not, I'm exactly right and so is she,' said Prince Florizel. 'Then when I saw her pulling faces and shouting insults and throwing princes to the ground, I knew she was the one person I could fall in love with.'

'Really?' asked the princess.

'Truly,' said Prince Florizel. 'Now, come and see my mechanical digger.'

And holding the oilcan in one hand and the princess's hand in the other, he led the way to the machine shed.

The king looked at Prince Florizel's father.

'There's nothing I can do with her once she's made up her mind,' he said wearily.

'I have the same trouble with Florizel,' said the second king. 'I say, would you like an Alka Seltzer and some breakfast?'

'Would I?' said the princess's father. 'I certainly would.'

So arm-in-arm they went off together to the palace.

And so Princess Ermyntrude and Prince Florizel were married in tremendous splendour.

The Princess Ermyntrude had a special diamond and gold thread boiler suit made for the wedding and she drove herself to the church in a beautiful bright red forklift truck with 'E' in flashing lights on one side and 'F' picked out in stars on the other and with garlands of flowers on the forks.

Prince Florizel, who had parachuted in for the wedding wore an emerald and silver thread shirt with silver lamé trousers and had flowers in his beard. On the steps of the church he reached up on tiptoe to kiss the princess as the television cameras whirred and the people cheered, then they ran down the steps and jumped into the royal forklift and steered away through the excited crowds.

'I'm terribly happy,' murmured the prince.

'So am I,' said the princess. 'I say, did you bring the hamburgers and the ketchup?'

'All there in the back,' said the prince.

'And I remembered the wedding cake. Look at it,' said the princess proudly.

'Good heavens,' cried Prince Florizel. 'It's magnificent.'

For the wedding cake was shaped like a giant oilcan.

'Perfect, don't you think?' murmured the princess.

'Absolutely,' said the prince.

And they both lived happily ever after.

SYNTE PEACOCK

The Secret Diary of Father Christmas, aged 57²/₇

1st December

I woke up from 'ibernation today. Been asleep since January. That's what I call a decent lie-in. Made a phone call to check up that me elves are still 'ard at work, makin' all the toys. I've got seventy million, nine hundred and thirty-six thousand, four hundred and eighty-one kids to deliver presents to this year. Just thinkin' about it makes me tired.

Tomorrow I'm auditioning reindeer for the sleigh. There are 'undreds of 'em milling about. I don't know why they are all so keen. It's 'ard work being Santa. You 'ave to arrange for every kid's record to be looked up, decide exactly what presents will be best for each one, and then get the elves to make them.

It looks bloomin' freezin' outside. Three feet of flamin' snow already. I want a green Christmas for a change. Bright sunshine and warm beaches. I can't stand the cold. It's all right for all them reindeer out there. They've got fur coats. Dunno why they 'ave to keep stickin' their noses up against my kitchen window. I can't even eat my breakfast in peace. And the fire in 'ere isn't warm enough. And the bread isn't fresh. And there is not enough bacon and only six eggs. And the coffee is 'alf cold. And the ice cream is mint instead of toffee fudge chocolate.

I'd 'ave given up this job years ago if it wasn't for the 'oliday. The pay is much too low – only £278 per child this year. The pressure is awful. It never stops. God I 'ate mint ice cream. Good thing there were only three tubs.

I 'ave to design the sleigh now. It's gonna have central 'eating this year.

It's gettin' dark. Four o'clock. It's been a long day. I'm already 'alf asleep. I'll design the sleigh tomorrow.

2nd December

I was woken up unbelievably early by the telephone. It was only 10 o'clock! It was the elves telling me that the felt-tip pen machine is jammed; it just keeps churning out millions of pens – all with yellow ink. I told 'em we'd give 'em as highlighter pens.

3rd December

Decided to audition the reindeer today; see 'ow fast they could run and 'ow 'igh they could jump. Every bloomin' reindeer in the country turned up. All two 'undred of 'em. Took me five and a 'alf hours to get through 'em all. I 'ad to hang about waiting for 'em to come back from the run I sent 'em on.

Then I chose the ones I always 'ave anyway: Donner, Blitzen, Prancer, Dancer, Cupid and Comet. Stupid names. And Rudolph, who came back last from the run 'cause 'e fell asleep in the kitchen, where he was 'iding. I only choose 'im because 'e can do 800 mph easily when 'e wants to. The Red Noses 'ave always been the fastest, but they are also the worst behaved.

I took 'em to the big shed they will be sleeping in this year, but Rudolph went ravin' mad; said it was too cold. I took the temperature in there. It was −32°C. I told 'im it was −1°C, which is warm for 'em. I 'ave to go and get 'em all some food now. I'll give 'em a packet of corn flakes. I 'ate corn flakes.

Just got back from feeding 'em. Instead of seven, there were two hundred packed in there trying to keep warm. What's worse is that all Rudolph's family are with 'im. Twelve Red Noses is more than I can stand. I've 'ad enough of them reindeer for now. They can do what they like, so long as they keep away from me.

I'll design the sleigh tomorrow.

4th December

I woke up this morning and found all the bloomin' reindeer asleep in *my* room, and Rudolph fast asleep on *my* bed with Sal. Just because my room has got central 'eating, and a fire, and it's big, they think they can sleep there, all two 'undred of them. I decided to kill 'em all – one by one – before they woke up.

I 'ad second thoughts about killing 'em. The foreman elf rang up and said they are falling behind with the presents, so I've got the reindeer busy making toys in my workshop now. I told 'em they could all sleep in there tonight.

5th December

Tired me out, all that bother yesterday. I suppose I'll 'ave to go down and see 'ow they are getting on. I bet Rudolph will find some way of skiving.

6th December

I went down to the workshops to see 'ow everything was goin'. Sal's had a baby. Rudolph's the father. Says 'e can't work because 'e 'as to look after the baby.

I told 'im I'd look after it and 'e bit my arm! He must have found out how I roll 'em downstairs and 'alf drown 'em when they're babies to toughen 'em up.

While Rudolph *was* working, guess what toys 'e and the others made. Tiny wooden red bloomin' nosed reindeer. They're all over everywhere.

I'll design that sleigh tomorrow.

10th December

I haven't written for a couple of days or so because I was designing the sleigh. In the end I decided to leave it the same except for extra food cupboards, extra heaters, and an extra long whip.

14th December

I've been carefully drawing up the list of presents for all the kiddies. All the A to Ms are getting yellow felt-tips and all the N to Zs are getting a wooden red nosed reindeer.

20th December

I 'aven't written for ages 'cause nowt much 'as happened. Even Rudolph has been behavin 'imself. I 'ope 'e 'as some more babies. It keeps him tired out.

Me dishwasher is bust thanks to Rudolph trying to wash Rudy, the baby, in it.

21st December

It gets colder every day. I'm dreading Christmas Eve. Only three days to go. I've got about 'alf a million more toys to make, I think.

All day I've been in the kitchen supervising the elves packing up sacks full of toys and loading 'em onto me sleigh. Me feet are killing me and I got really cold opening the window to shout at 'em all the time.

I 'ate Christmas Eve. Most of the adults are so mean, although most kids leave me some biscuits or cake or wine by the Christmas tree. I always give 'em whatever they ask for on their list – if I've got it with me. Otherwise they get an extra pair of socks. But some 'ouses 'ave notices saying things like 'Father Christmas is only a story' or 'I don't believe in Santa'. Then I don't give 'em anything. I take *away* all their presents.

22nd December

A man from the NSPCR came round today. NSPCR stands for National Society for the Prevention of Cruelty to Reindeer. 'E fined me £2,000 because 'e said I wasn't feeding the reindeer properly and was making 'em work too hard. I paid 'im off with Monopoly money.

Some carol singers came round last night. I gave 'em Rudy, the baby. 'E's even worse than 'is father. I was glad to get rid of 'im, but somehow 'e got back and was curled up at the bottom of my bed this morning as usual. I'm gonna kill that whole family of Red Noses one day.

I watched the *Superman* films all in a row today. They were brilliant, except for *Superman II*; all that snow and ice made me feel cold.

23rd December

Been making last minute preparations, like filling up the sleigh with food. I've made every present now so I'm 'aving a bit of a rest at last. 'Bout time too. Me feet are killing me after all the rushing about for the past 22 days.

There's about two metres of snow outside. Don't know 'ow the reindeer can stand it. Probably 'cause they spend most of their time sleeping in me bedroom.

I've been looking everywhere for me Santa uniform, but I can only find the trousers and coat. I don't know where the beard is.

Better go to bed now or I'll never wake up in time tomorrow.

24th December

Well, I've delivered about 'alf the presents so far. I'm in Germany and I'm lost. The reindeer don't know where to go and all the road signs are in a bloomin' foreign language.

I got stuck in one chimney and it took me ages to get out. Rudolph said it's probably 'cause I'm so fat! I'm gonna sack 'im when we get back 'ome.

One 'ouse I went to 'ad a table full of grub. There were eight plates, glasses, knives, forks, spoons, and napkins, and a bottle of wine, a big turkey, all sorts of vegetables, some nice sauce, a bowl of roast potatoes, some fruit, and this lovely big chocolate cake. I knew they must 'ave left the meal for me, so I ate it all. I don't know why they set eight places. Maybe they thought I'd let the reindeer 'ave something to eat. Anyway, it was a lovely meal, especially the turkey and the chocolate. Pity there wasn't any ice cream, though.

In another 'ouse, I saw all these presents on a table saying 'Love from Father Christmas' on them. I knew they must 'ave made a mistake and put 'from' instead of 'to'. Some people! Good thing I can think for myself. I took 'em and they were these boxes of lovely vanilla fudge. It didn't take me long to get through 'em.

In one 'ouse I found a letter. It said:

> Dear Father Christmas,
> When you come tonight please will you leave me an electric guitar, a grand piano, a horse, a reindeer, three dogs, seven cats, a hi-fi system, a colour TV, a video recorder, a computer, and whatever else you like. If

you leave these things you can have the big box of toffees under this note.
Lots of love,
Jason.

I took the toffees and gave 'im a packet of yellow felt-tips.

I 'aven't seen anyone yet and I don't want to because I found me beard last night. Or half of it. Rudy had been chewing it. I feel a right moron walking around with 'alf a beard.

25th December
Got back 'ome about 3 a.m. It was freezing cold and icicles were hanging from my nose. The temperature was −38°C.

Woke up this afternoon. There was a present for me from Rudolph. It was a picture of all the bloomin' Red Noses in the country. Rudolph said it would keep me happy on long, boring evenings. From the elves I got a barrel of ice cream. Mint!

'Ad a lovely Christmas dinner, though. A big turkey, gravy, sprouts, cauliflower, crisp roast potatoes, beer or wine (I 'ad both), and as much of everything as I wanted.

It's nearly 9 p.m. now, and I feel like being sick. I should go out and feed the reindeer, but I think I'll give it a miss tonight. Nice Christmas present for 'em. I'm gonna go and 'ibernate till next Christmas now.

Merry Christmas!

Beautiful Tara

That same week, two major events occurred.

First, the Corn Circles, the rings in the field. You know what I mean: here's the big field, a sea of growing corn rippling in the breeze: then the circles are suddenly there, a pattern of circles like this:

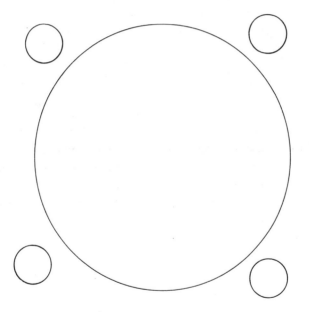

Perfect circles! The big, central one looks as if it were made by letting down from a sky-hook a vast rotary lawnmower, 50 metres wide. The outer circles are about seven metres across, and again, perfect. Razor-sharp edges, flattened discs of corn.

They came in the night. Everyone in our village went to gawp next day. TV and newspaper people arrived; and scientists, beardy weirdos with theories, the lot.

Our circle wasn't unique. You've seen and read stories about other circles. But as I say, ours was a cracker, a perfect specimen.

Then another perfect specimen arrived from nowhere. Tara.
Tara.
I can't find the words to describe her. She was the most beautiful girl ever, that's all. Her face, features, figure – all perfect. And then, her smile. Sweet, luminous, sexy, innocent . . . perfect.
Radiant, that's the word I want. Tara was radiant. She moved in a golden circle of joy, welcome, aliveness. Yet this same ring guarded her. Somehow it told you to keep your distance.

Guess who got her. Right, first time. Neil, our teenage star, king of everything in our school from aerobics to Social Studies. Neil, taking A level Maths at 15. And exactly six feet tall, of course. He got her. He and Tara were always together. The rest of us turned green with envy and whimpered like puppies. Especially me. If Neil wasn't one of my best friends, I could have killed him. Hell, I could have killed him anyhow if it got me Tara.

Neil's father runs a Shire horse stables. Like son, like father: Neil's dad is a big success, complete with Range Rover, BMW and red sports car for the little woman. Neil will take over the sports car when he's older. Meanwhile, he makes do with a 12-speed lightweight with chrome forks, hand-made.
And Tara, of course.

So there they were, the two of them, close as two sticks.
No, wait, that's not quite true. They weren't all that close physically. You never saw them smooch, or twine round each other at the disco. They didn't even link arms. But I told you about that earlier, didn't I? Touch-me-not Tara. It didn't affect their happiness.

One day I went with them, on my old four-speed banger, to visit the Shire horses. I had my camera. I took pictures, nearly all of Tara with her smiling face uplifted, her gorgeous bust jutting, her hair blowing.

I use black and white. I like doing blow-ups. I did one of Tara's smile, mouth wide open to show her perfect teeth.

I mean, *perfect*. Not one filling, which is interesting.

Another interesting thing – in several photos, she rests her hand on the shoulder or neck of a horse. Now, Shire horses are as powerful as King Kong and as gentle as babies. And they understand people, they bow their heads so that people in wheelchairs can reach their heads. I love to touch them, you get good vibes. So did Tara.

Yet after the first pat or two from her, the horse would sort of flinch. Its hide would flicker, its head would swing away. I thought nothing of it at the time.

Neil got ill. He stayed away from school. I met his dad in the High Street and asked, 'What's the trouble?'

'Nothing in particular. The Doctor can't find anything. He's just . . . under the weather.' He smiled but looked worried.

I said, 'We visited your horses the other day. Aren't they great!'

He said, 'Well, there we go again. Three of *them* are sick, just like Neil. Off their oats. Can't understand it.'

I said I was sorry and he shrugged and waved his hand and drove off.

Neil ill, horses ill. Still I didn't see the light. But how could I have done?

Neil was off ill, so I stepped in. I took over where he left off with Tara.

It was like winning the pools, being top of the pops and getting knighted, rolled into one. Just being *seen* with her was an all-time high.

I know what you want to ask. The answer is, no, we didn't, not in any sense or degree. Badminton, swimming, discos, take your pick. We did it all. But never the other.

As if I cared! Just being with her was enough. Radiant, she was radiant! She radiated like a sun lamp – no, like the sun itself. I basked.

But too much sun can be bad for you.

After a week or so with Tara, I got all the classic sunburn

symptoms except the burn. I felt tired, lifeless, achey, flat, drained.

Drained. Good old me, sometimes I pick just the right word . . .

Now, some more about the Corn Circles.

The TV people and helicopters lost interest. A few of the beardy weirdos stayed on. They spent a lot of time talking to old Freddie, our village character. They took him seriously and he took them for pint after pint.

'Arrr!' he told them, 'Oi was *thurrrr*, roight enough, the noight it came and made them shapes in noine-acre field!' (All right, I'll cut out the accent.)

'Like a red light in the sky, it were,' he told them. 'Like a storm brewing, but no lightning, no wind, no rain. Then a great *shape*, with lines of fire coming down from it like stair rods, and a sound like you never heard!'

He made a sound like a constipated vacuum-cleaner. The beardy lot made notes and tape recordings, all very earnest.

Codswallop, of course – except for one thing: old Freddie could have been out that night. And most other nights too. He's an old-style poacher, you see. He goes for birds, salmon – whatever the hotels and restaurants will pay for. He's even got a metal detector. He found Tara's ring with it.

I gave her that ring. It cost me my savings. I gave it to her because it was bright, beautiful, radiant. And because I wanted her to melt into my manly arms and murmur 'Take me!!!'

Some chance. She never let me see her home, even. At the village hall, she'd say, 'Till tomorrow then!' and throw a smile that lit up the dark – then pedal away. She explained it by telling me that her parents were abroad, she was temporarily stuck with a loony old aunt in a horrible little house. No visitors.

I didn't argue. Anyhow, I gave her the ring and she made the right 'Oooo' noises and I thought 'Aha! The moment has come!' So I thrust myself at her, falling over my bike on the way, and got her in a gorilla grip, aiming my lips at her face.

She didn't resist. To my surprise, my lips made a direct hit on hers.

To my greater surprise, she said 'Mmmm!' and returned my kiss. She put her arms round my neck and kissed me. I felt a rocket go up my spine. My brain turned to jelly. Steam jetted out of my ears.

She lightened her grip and kissed me again. My knees buckled.

You think I'm trying to write about red hot romance? Wrong. It *hurt*. I felt as if I had been mugged, clubbed, wrung out like a rag.

I had to walk my bike home, I couldn't ride it.

I stayed in bed for three days.

So I missed the third major event: Tara's disappearance.

And the fourth: the appearance of another set of Corn Circles, identical to the first and almost in the same place.

I could take or leave the Corn Circles; they didn't interest me much. But no more Tara . . .

And, as the Police and the school discovered, no loony old aunt: no horrible little house. Tara had lived nowhere with no-one.

I've worked it all out. The ring gave me what must be the answer.

As you can imagine, the new Corn Circles stirred everything up again. More TV and press people, more helicopters, more scientists with more gear measuring everything from circumferences to magnetic impulses, more beardy weirdos with theories. Every centimetre of the ground was covered.

Yet it was old Freddie who found the ring. That evening, when everyone else had packed it in, he was out there with his metal detector and I chanced to be there with him. He looked at the ground searching for treasure. I looked at the sky yearning for Tara.

He found the ring. *Her* ring. And, because it was twisted, blackened, charred, valueless, he let me have it.

I held it in the palm of my hand and felt sick. What went wrong, I wonder? Did they snatch up Tara in some sort of panic, and mutilate her?

Or didn't they care about her? Was she just a piece of used

equipment to be sent to some scrapyard in infinite space?

Yes, I've worked it all out, I think. I'll tell *you*, but not the newspaper people or the authorities or anyone like that. I don't like people laughing at me.

Tara was a fuel agency.

Cars run on petrol, milk floats on electricity. And so on and so on. What do spaceships that make Corn Circles run on? My guess is, animal energy.

Suppose that whatever place the spaceships come from has run out of energy sources, just as we may run out of coal or oil. Suppose they have to visit other planets to find the energy they need.

Horses, young humans, even a dog that likes to be patted – there's the energy source. And Tara was the beautifully-made collection and storage cell.

Succuba. You've never met that word, have you? It took me days to find it. In the public library. A Succuba was a female sucker of energy, a sort of female vampire. Stories of Succubae go right back through history. But then, so do stories about spaceships.

Tara, you were so beautiful! But you were just a *thing*, an agent, a parasite. Don't ever come back.

No, Tara! Please come back and let me see you smile again!

Master of the Universe

Martin attempted to brush his dark hair back the way it was before his mother had ruffled it. He didn't like being touched, not by her or anyone else, but especially not by her.

'Go on, Martin, clean the animal out before the daylight goes,' she had said smiling at him over the top of her stupid new glasses. He wanted her to leave him alone. He wanted to be rid of that animal too.

He wrinkled his nose as he peered into the stinking cage. Not that he could see much inside Grampa's gloomy shed. He didn't need to see; his nose told him everything he needed to know. Rotting carrots, flabbing lettuce and stinking wet sawdust.

'You stinking little pig!' he hissed with as much venom as he could. The chirrup of a friendly guinea pig was his answer.

A beam of sunlight poked into the shed just then. Dust and small flies flew in it. Like a spotlight in a theatre, it lit up a circular patch on the floor of the cage . . . and He-man, sensing his moment, arrived.

There were no two ways about it, He-man was a disgusting animal. One ear and one eye (courtesy of Caesar, next door's ginger Tom), a large scabby lump on his side, and more bald patches than black fur.

'You are revolting! Time for you to die!' Martin wrenched open the cage door, sending He-man skittering around, squirting bursts of sawdust. He tossed in a carrot, as if it were a grenade, and swung the door shut.

'Bye, bye, pig. Bang! Splat!'

Thursday was pension day. Martin always liked to walk ten or twelve yards ahead of his grandfather, which was easy because his grandfather would have trouble out-pacing a slug. Every so often Martin would stop and wait for the old man, who would shuffle, head nodding, mouth making his normal noise, 'bompadompadomp,bompadompadomp', towards him. Martin had no idea what that noise meant. It was as if his grandfather's tongue and legs were joined together in some way. He couldn't do one thing without the other. It was just another embarrassing thing he had to put up with. It wasn't the worst though. Martin tried to arrange the embarrassing things in rank order:

Grandpa smelt of trousers, like those five pound notes that smell like they have been in a tramp's pocket for years.

Grandpa wore both belt and braces, and his trousers were so short that the turnups flapped around stilton coloured shins, so he looked like a tramp, too.

He would sing 'On Mother Kelly's Doorstep' suddenly in the middle of meals, or worse, in public.

He would insist on washing up, but would leave bits of fish on the forks.

He rubbed his maroon leather slippers together when he watched television. It made an irritating creaking noise, and after a while Martin would find himself listening to that instead of the television.

He went bompadompadomp, bompadompadomp, all the time.

His grandfather, wheezing, drew up to him.

'. . . bompadompadomp . . . You'll be old yourself one day. How about slowing down a bit and giving a poor old soul a bit of company, eh? That's why Doreen sends you with me.' The last words turned into a wheeze, then some bubbling and finally into a blob of green spat onto the curb.

Martin looked at him, then looked up and down the road. It was a long line of pre-war terraces with cracking chimneys and sagging television aerials. It was old, boring. He knew that keeping the old man company wasn't why his mother, Doreen (what a stupid name that was), sent him with his Grandfather. She told him that it was so he could look after the old man, get him across roads and protect him from muggers. 'A boy of your age needs responsibility,' she said brushing back his hair and poking the label down the back of his sweater. He wasn't fooled; it was part of her plan to embarrass him at all possible times. Why else would she send him with this thing out in public? Why else would she make them live in grandfather's tatty house with no car and just a black and white TV? Why else would she wear jeans and no make-up? None of this would have happened if his dad hadn't . . . His grandfather belched, spat and opened his tobacco tin.

'You're not supposed to smoke,' he snapped, his voice shooting up an octave half way through the sentence. 'The doctor said so.'

'What'll it do, shorten me life expectancy? I'm eighty-four, you know.' Grandfather lit a roll-up, drew smoke deep into his lungs, then coughed a cough that made his whole body shake.

'I'd heard a rumour.' It was meant to be sarky but it came out in the little boy half of his voice. If he was honest with himself he was frightened that his grandfather wouldn't stop coughing.

Martin lay on his bed in a Sunday mood. A train rattled at the bottom of the garden and the odd spot of rain tapped on the glass. The roast beef and Yorkshire pud was too big for his stomach and he had a greasy and sour layer over his teeth and tongue. It was Sunday. He hated Sundays. Sundays meant nothing going on, drizzly weather, too much food, bad telly and cleaning out bloody He-man. Why did he have to be saddled with such a ridiculous animal? Why couldn't he have a Siberian husky? Even a garter snake had something. A guinea pig, a cavy, a clapped out, geriatric, scabby, incontinent rodent. Naff, naff, naff! A little voice said in his brain, 'Because you asked for it brainiack, that's why! Don't you remember?'

Of course he did remember. Martin Scully, No. 1 Rodent Keeper at All Saints Primary. Every break, carrots. ('Can I have a guinea pig, Mum?') Every lunchtime, lettuce. ('Can I have a guinea pig, Dad?') Every holiday, carrying the cage home and tending them. ('Can I have a guinea pig, Muuuuum?' 'Oh, all right, but you'll have to look after it and clean it out.' 'Course I will, thank you Mum!')

He got two for the price of one at the pet shop. He could still remember letting the two bean-shaped creatures out of their cardboard carrying box into the new cage. They skittered round then froze, breathing hard, an image of a smiling boy in each of their ink drop eyes.

He called them He-man and She-ra because Tully Fresno, the American kid in his class, had held Martin spellbound with his descriptions of the adventures of these characters from an American cartoon series.

He smiled as he lay on his bed, the rain raining just enough to run down the window. The Masters of the Universe cartoon was now on British TV; Martin thought it was rubbish. He had been so happy with those useless creatures with their pathetic names. Happiness was two warm rodents. Life would never be that simple again.

He came home from school that day. The two creatures were in their wire mesh run on the lawn. She-ra sat in a patch of sun, head up, hypnotised. He-man sat in the water dish looking uncomfortable and confused. He squeaked at them and they jumped and rushed to opposite ends of the pan. He could remember even then feeling a stab of annoyance at their lack of brain. He bent to stroke one through the wire; his mother rushed from the house with eyeshadow half-way down her face. She fell on him, bound him with her arms and legs and wailed. She smelt like the seaside.

His Dad was dead.

In the hours that had followed, he had numbly followed people he sort of knew, had his hair ruffled, been given numerous cups of tea that he hadn't drunk, and a glass of whisky which he had then coughed all over the carpet. When he had cried finally, somebody had said, 'Be strong for your mother. You're the man of the house now.' He'd stopped then and never cried since, although he'd tried.

It wasn't until much later he remembered the guinea pigs. The sun had been strong all that day and still was, even though it was late evening. When he arrived at the run, She-rah lay on her side, her eyes crusted but open. He knew she was dead. He-man was hunched into the only bit of shadow there was, one of the wooden supports of the pen.

With the shadow up his back and his orange sides sticking out, He-man looked like a Liquorice Allsort, the kind nobody likes. The creature had its eyes closed and was breathing very fast. Martin scooped the panting creature up.

Martin filled the kitchen sink up with cold water and put He-man in it. Somebody or other told him that it was no time to play with the pets.

'I can't just let him die!' he had shouted. 'Life must go on!' He didn't know why he said the last thing. Someone had said it to him earlier. His mother had looked at him, shocked.

The cold water brought He-man round enough to bite Martin on the thumb. Martin dried him with a tea-towel and returned him to the cage. He-man had circled, making little grumbling noises and, Martin thought, looked at him reproachfully, 'I'm sorry about She-rah, He-man, but life must go on.'

And it had, after a fashion.

His dad was dead. His dad was dead. He wondered if he'd ever get used to that sentence. He'd had to get used to the effects of it. It was why he and his mum lived with his senile old fool of a grandfather. It was why his bedroom was decorated with wallpaper with spacemen and rockets. ('Don't you dare say anything to him about it, Martin. You hear me? He thought that's what boys liked. It isn't easy decorating at his age.''He shouldn't have bothered.' 'Not another word!') It was why he had no pocket money; why they had no car; why . . . everything. Sundays! He listened to the telly booming downstairs, his grandfather laughing and coughing, the clank of washing-up, the train rattle in the distance, the rain rattle on the window. His dad was dead. He waited.

About half an hour later the call came.

'Martin!'

'Yes, Mum? Get lost.' The last under his breath.

'Are you going to clean He-man out?'

'I'm doing my homework.' He hastily hid his motorcycle mag.

'I'm pleased to hear it, but that can wait for a bit. You've got to do the animal before the light goes.' Her voice echoed

strangely in the landing, deeper and older than usual.
He passed her on the way out to the shed. She ruffled his
hair. She had to reach up to do it. He shrugged out from under
her hand. 'Don't!' he said. He turned to catch a sad expression
on her face. She looked like that a lot lately. He didn't like the
way she looked since Dad died (there it was again), with her
short hair, jeans and long earrings with wooden beads on.
She said it was practical and comfortable. She'd never looked
uncomfortable to him before . . .

'Be nice for once,' she said to his back. He pretended he
hadn't heard.

The sun had come out and Grampa was on slug patrol. It
was another of his revolting habits. Singing tunelessly he
prowled his rows of broad beans, cabbages, marrows and his
patches of strawberries, the sunlight glinting on his watch-
chain, glasses' frames and the blades of the long garden
scissors he carried. When he found a slug he would chuckle,
'Gotcha!' and snip the animal in two with the scissors then
wipe the blades clean on his trousers. Disgusting!

Martin looked at the house to either side to make sure no
one was looking at him while his grandfather was around.

'Oh, so you're out then?' said the old man from behind
some French beans.

'No it's an illusion. What do you think?'

'I think you're not as clever as you think you are.' For some
reason, although he'd heard exactly those words a thousand
times, this time they got through and stung a little. He was
glad for once, to reach the smelly interior of the shed.

That evening he sat on the floor, leaning his back against the
sofa. His mum sat to his left and his grandfather to his right,
they passed a box of Liquorice Allsorts over his head while
they watched *That's Life*. On the flickering blue screen a group
of hospital cleaners were singing a song about bedpans, while
some others played tunes on surgical instruments. Martin
squirmed at the stupidity of adults. His mum looked amused
over the top of her new glasses and grandpa wheezed,
squeaked and slapped his leg. When he stopped slapping, he
went back to rubbing his slippers together; it made a loud

squeaky creaking. Martin felt his eyes constantly pulled towards the maroon leather slippers moving over each other squeaking, felt his irritation growing.

'There's plenty of room on the seat, son; you can't sit on the floor!' Grandfather meant to tap him gently on the shoulder but accidentally poked him in the ear instead. Martin exploded.

'Leave me alone you silly old fool, just leave me alone!' Even he was surprised at his own violence. His voice didn't crack either. It all came out in a vicious low growl. He slammed the door as he ran out.

He lay on his bed with the light out. He could hear the news through the floor and a fire-engine in the distance. He felt like a snake must feel when it needs to shed its skin. Every inch of his skin felt stretched and ready to tear and his insides felt explosive. Something had to give.

There was a light tap at the door.

'Martin? Can I come in?'

He had expected her to be angry but her voice was soft. For some reason this was worse.

'Martin?'

'What?'

'Can I come in?'

'If you want.' He rolled towards the wall, saw the spacemen on the wall, and rolled back angrily. She came in. She didn't turn the light on, but left the door open so that the light from the hallway slanted gently in. She knelt by his bed and put a hand on his arm. He clenched the muscle to make the arm hard, but she didn't take her hand away.

'You can't go on like this, Martin. It's not fair on Grandad and me. I know it's been hard on you, but we do the best we can.'

He stared at the ceiling and tried to keep his throat still, while something sharp tore it in half.

'We have a right to live, too, Martin . . .'

'So live,' he croaked out.

She ignored this. 'It's like nothing we do or say pleases you, like we're nuisances all the time. You never talk to us.' Her voice was still gentle, but it began to have an edge of pleading, of control.

'I've got nothing to say. Just want to be left alone, that's all.' As he said it, he knew that wasn't it at all. He didn't want to be left alone at all, he wanted his . . .

'We all miss your father, Martin, you forget that.' Her words touched a spot too raw for him to take. He turned to the spaceman wallpaper. She got up and looked at him from where she stood.

'I can't talk to you anymore. You're selfish. I can't talk to you. You don't think of anyone but yourself.' Her voice was sad and gentle, but hard and steady too. 'I can't talk to you, Martin. You can't even be bothered to look after that poor animal of yours any more. You've got no time for any one of us, have you?'

His mouth attempted to tremble round something, but the door was closed on him. For the first time since that day, he felt tears on his cheek. They burned down his burning cheeks as the television boomed beneath the floor.

The sun was honey coloured and the scent of grass waggled the hair up his nose. He looked up into the light to make himself sneeze. He did. He-man in his pen on the lawn did a vertical take-off, then rushed from one end to the other, via his water dish. Then he froze and panted for a while, then began nibbling the grass again as if nothing had happened.

'Stupid animal,' said Martin and thrust a glowing carrot through the wire.

A train rattled along in the distance, and a plane throbbed overhead. His mother was starfished on a lounger, her jeans rolled up, her toes pointing upwards, a book in one hand and sunglasses in the other, both hands trailing on the grass. Grandfather was amongst his raspberry canes with a pair of pruning shears. Martin could hear him mumbling and breathing words from songs, occasionally interspersed with 'bompadompadomp' and clip of the shears.

Martin looked along the row of houses with their different paint-work and arrangements of pipes. All the different TV aerials. The different gardens. Different windows. Lives.

Grandfather faced him further down the path. He waved with one hand, while scratching his bum with the other. 'You all right, boy?'

'Yes, ta!' His mother jerked awake then fell asleep again, her glasses dropping out of her grasp.

'There are some big slugs down here, come and have a look!' The old man gestured with the shears.

'Later!' laughed Martin.

'There is no later for them.' The blades caught the light, threw it in Martin's eyes for a moment and then grandfather turned his back.

He-man was basking in a patch of sun, his black fur bleaching orange. His sides panted in and out and he made little chirruping noises of pleasure. His tattered ears, and scabby sides didn't look so bad out in the sun and his eye shone with brainless rodent fire.

The flash of light from the blades. The sunglasses on the grass. The different windows of the houses. The happy rodent . . . and Martin.

Another train passed, going somewhere. His grandfather appeared to listen for a moment then muttered, 'Bompadompadomp.'

So that was it.

DAVID HARMER

The Shrimp

The little kid had been crying. Me and Pritchard found him
down by the power station. He was scrunched up in a ball by
the edge of one of the slurry pits. His face was all red and
streaky. I was surprised to see him there. It's a dangerous
place.

We walked over to him. Pritchard picked him up. The kid
began to thrash about. 'Get off,' he shouted. 'Get off me.'

Pritchard just laughed and held him by his coat collar, even
tighter than before. The kid squirmed and pushed. He tried to
kick Pritchard, but he just held the kid at arm's length laughing loudly. The kid was trying to speak but he couldn't. His
breath came out in grunts as he wrestled with Pritchard.
Pritchard's big. Tall. He's got a long reach. The kid didn't
stand a chance.

He was a skinny kid. About ten or eleven with a pointed
face. He had blonde hair and his ears stuck out. So did his
teeth.

'Hey, Fozzy,' Pritchard said.

'What?' I said.

'He looks like one of those elves.'

'What elves?' I said.

'The ones in town. The ones stuck round Santa's sledge. On
that model.'

He was right. We both laughed and the little kid wriggled
about. Pritchard still had hold of his coat collar and the kid
was going red, trying to break loose.

'Now he looks like a shrimp,' I said, 'all skinny and pink.'

'Leave me alone,' he squealed.

'Sorry, shrimp,' Pritchard laughed and dropped him so that
he rolled towards the slurry pit. But only a little way. He got
up and dusted himself.

'Stop picking on me,' he shouted and a great fat tear rolled down his pointy little face.

'Aren't you scared of us two?' asked Pritchard. 'We're big us two. Bigger than you.'

'No,' sniffed the kid. 'I'd be more scared of a rice pudding.'

I thought Pritchard was going to belt him then. You can never tell with Pritchard. You can't predict his next move. This time he just laughed. 'Hear that, Fozzer? Cheeky monkey.'

'If you're not scared of us, why are you crying?' I asked him.

'It's me dog,' he sniffed, 'our Lulu.'

'Lulu!' Pritchard howled. 'What kind of a name is that for a dog?'

The kid shrugged 'I don't know. Me mum called her it. Lulu.'

'What's up with the dog, then?' I said.

He pointed past us, over our shoulders towards the lagoons. 'She's in there,' he said. 'She ran off and fell in there. Going for a stick. She's drowned.'

I looked. I could see the power station about half a mile away. Then I looked at the big lakes of thick chalky lime slurry stretched out in front of us. If you fell in one of them you wouldn't touch bottom. You'd just sink. Like quicksand.

'Look,' said Pritchard, 'look there, Fozzer. It's the dog.'

He was pointing to something floating on the surface. At first I thought he was wrong. It looked like a lump of wood. A tiny blob of wood lying there, too light to sink through the creamy slime. I looked harder. It had eyes. They were only just open. And it had a mouth. I could see it was a dog now. It tried to bark. It was struggling to swim but it couldn't, nothing could move through that sticky mess. As we looked it disappeared, just vanished.

'No,' shouted Pritchard. 'No.'

'Stop!' I yelled, but he was off, racing round the lake to where the head had suddenly showed up again through the lumpy surface.

'Lulu!' the shrimp shouted.

I just got him in time as he went to leap in after his dog. We fell down and I grabbed him. He began to yell and thrash about, but I didn't let go.

'Get off,' he screamed, 'you murderer! You dog killer!'

'Shut up,' I said, 'or I'll murder you.'

He calmed down a bit, so I let go. He sat up. He didn't try it again. He was covered in cement dust and his face was filthy. I turned round and we both watched Pritchard.

He was near the dog now. He was flat on his stomach, trying to reach out to the tiny bit of the dog's head that showed above the level of the slurry. He stood up and shouted me over.

'Stop here, shrimp,' I said. He didn't. He just followed me. 'Grab hold of my belt,' said Pritchard. He sat down in front of me and stuck his legs into the lake. The white slime oozed around them. I could hear it slither and gurgle.

'Hold on, Foz,' he shouted. 'Here I go!'

I got hold tight of his belt and he just dropped forwards into the lake. For one terrible moment I thought he'd take me with him, but I clung on and pulled him back. He looked as if he was swimming in thick cream paint. He had his arms stretched out. The little kid was going barmy.

'Lulu,' he shouted, 'come on, girl.'

Pritchard stretched out and almost dragged me in again. But he got the dog. He got a hold on its collar and he tugged. I pulled backwards and the three of us landed in a big slippery mess on the side of the lake.

The dog was a big one. It could hardly move. It was caked in slurry. It was tired out by its struggle to stay breathing. Pritchard was the same. He was coated top to toe in the stuff. His best jeans, trainers, everything. He bent down and stroked the dog. The dog managed a short flap of its tail.

The shrimp was hopping about in excitement. 'We've saved her, we've saved her,' he kept shouting. Then he wrapped his arms round the dog and hugged it.

'*We've* saved her?' Pritchard said. 'What did you do?'

'I had hold of him when he had hold of you,' said the kid, pointing at me. 'I held Fozzer's belt.'

'Oh, did you?' I said.

'Yeh,' he said. 'Good job, too. You nearly went in.'

He walked off. Lulu followed him, tottering along, drip-

ping wet and covered in runny cement. I looked at Pritchard. He was in a real state.

'You don't get a lot of thanks, do you?' he said, spitting out a mouthful of slurry.

'Good job it wasn't a Rottweiler,' I said. 'It might've bitten you.'

'Good job it wasn't an elephant,' said Pritchard. 'It might've drowned me.'

He can be like that can Pritchard.

Just Testing

Rob's house backed on to a park, and sometimes when it rained, it rained tiny frogs. Thousands of them, covering the street so that the tarmac seethed. Rob didn't know why this should happen, but it did. When the buses drove by, it sounded like millions of pop-guns going off, and when Rob walked to the shop he couldn't avoid the squelching.

So he grew up hating frogs. Also there was one morning at Cub camp. The Leader had it in his head that it was good for boys not to wear socks. So on wet days they had to wear Wellingtons on bare feet. This was a pretty clammy feeling in itself, but nothing to what Rob felt one rainy morning when he crawled out of his tent, plunged his naked foot into his Wellington, and experienced squashed frog seeping up between his toes.

This wasn't the frog's fault, of course, yet Rob never got over it, and always blamed the frog. So the relationship between Rob and frogs was that between squasher and squashee.

There's not going to be much more about frogs in this story, but there's a reason for starting with them. At the age of twelve Rob was presented with a choice. He wanted to join a gang. Pete and Tom's gang. It was a gang of two, and so it was really a big deal when they asked Rob to make it a gang of three. Most of the other boys looked up to Pete and Tom, who'd never before asked anyone to join them.

'But there's one thing you have to do,' Pete added, looking sideways at Tom with a smug, sly expression.

There was, it seemed, a test Rob had to go through to become a full gang member. He had to do one of three things. He had either to catch a frog and put it inside his mouth, preferably without his teeth crunching it, though that didn't matter. Or he had to catch, kill, cook and eat a pigeon. Or he had to catch a slowworm. Rob thought the last sounded easy. Anyone could catch a worm, especially if it was a slow sort. Then Pete explained it wasn't a worm at all, but a lizard-like creature, and that there were hundreds in his large garden on the hillside. Oh, and when Rob had caught one, he had to tie it into a reef knot around his neck.

Rob thought perhaps he didn't care about being a gang member after all. He'd never met a slowworm, but didn't much like the sound of them, especially in connexion with reef knots around his neck. He had met frogs, somehow nearly always in connection with feet. And as for pigeons – they were all right in their place, but their place wasn't inside Rob's stomach.

Yet he knew he did want to join. Deep inside himself he knew he'd got to. Tom and Pete each lived in a large house and their way of life was different from Rob's. The small council house he'd always lived in quite happily seemed cramped now, compared with their houses. What his mum and dad talked about seemed drab compared with what Tom and Pete's parents called 'conversation'.

This new world seemed much larger and he wanted to join it.

But put a frog in his mouth? No. Imagine it flobbing around on top of his tongue. Tie a slowworm around his neck, then? Shudder. But yes.

Pete showed him which part of the garden the slowworms liked. They slid and wriggled there in bliss. Rob wasn't in bliss when he saw them. He'd never seen anything like them. There was no room for creatures like this in his family's trim little vegetable garden. They'd have been told to wipe their feet before slithering across those neat rows of carrots and peas.

Rob didn't know slowworms were rather short of feet. He knew very little about the animal world at all, which for him consisted of: one, Sandy, his cat; two, next-door's dog that left big turds on their grass and was not well liked; three, frogs, to be avoided; four, birds, brown things up in the air, easily ignored, unless one broke its leg and you had to pick it up in a tea-cloth, drop it in a cardboard box and give it to somebody who could make it go out of your life; five, cows that munched in the park and left bigger, smellier turds than the dog but at least it wasn't on the family grass; six, the rabbits which you cleaned out with a trowel and a wrinkled nose, and which you ate at Christmas; seven, more frogs, to be avoided; eight, slugs, to be chopped up with a hoe, a job he often botched because he did it with his eyes closed.

Rob liked nature and animals, but he felt they should always be the other side of the fence. And now into his world squirmed slowworms, grey and alien, to be tied in a reef knot around his neck.

'I think it'd be more of a challenge if I did the pigeon thing. Eating it and that.'

Pete told him where to find pigeons. Pete knew everything. In the loft of an old outhouse on a nearby farm. Rob'd have to do the job himself, he said, and bring the dead bird back as proof – uncooked.

The outhouse was easy to find. Rob was a good climber and easily shinned up the thick prop to the loft. He grazed his thighs doing it, for this was in the days when boys of twelve wore short trousers, but he was used to this sort of injury and hardly noticed it. What he did notice was the slimy bird mess he plunged his hands into as soon as he hooked them over the ledge of the opening into the loft, to haul himself up the last few feet.

A surprise awaited him. There was only one pigeon there. One pigeon and all that mess? He didn't know or care. One was enough. Too many.

He crouched by the opening. He told himself this was to get his breath back, but really it was because he didn't want to do the next bit. So he crouched back, his eyes gradually getting used to the gloom.

One pigeon. He gazed at it. The bird didn't gaze back, but pecked, pecked, pecked in the filthy straw that littered the loft floor. Stupid bird. Might as well be dead, if that's all it does.

Rob went on crouching. Now the grazes on his thighs stung. He wiped the pigeon mess off his hands on to the seat of his shorts, but immediately put his hands into some more. It was everywhere. He was aware how much he was sweating, though it wasn't very warm.

He was a town boy, and the only place he'd seen pigeons before was at the bus station, where their oily colour matched the petrol stains on the concrete. He'd never thought about them, but now he tried to.

He just saw the bird's beady eye and easily breakable legs. He moved nearer, still crouching, balancing on the wooden beams so that he wouldn't crash through the floor. The bird stopped pecking. Rob did another crouching waddle towards it. The bird watched. Why doesn't the stupid thing fly off, out of my reach? The bird watched. Beady eye. Rob's shirt stuck to him with sweat. He tensed, to leap, grab and strangle.

In fact, he leapt to miss. Leapt into mess, while the bird easily hopped off a few yards. The words Rob said out loud weren't the ones that Pete's parents called conversation, though he'd often heard them shouted by his own mum at his dad, and by his dad at his mum, before they made up again. Between their noisy squabbles, his mum and dad loved one another strongly.

All this passed through Rob's brain as he crouched in the pigeon mess, sweating with frustration. He didn't know what to do. He lurched forward another pace towards the bird, always crouching, so that his thighs began to ache as well as sting.

He thought of Pete's house. Rich carpets. Grand piano. Rob's house had lino. It did have a piano, but battered and tiny. His mum sometimes played 'Bye bye, blackbird' on it. 'There'll be bluebirds over the white cliffs of Dover.' 'When the red red robin comes bob bob bobbin' along.' 'If I were a blackbird I'd whistle and sing.'

But she'd never played anything about pigeons.

He leapt. Caught the bird between his two amazed hands. It throbbed but could do nothing. His hands slid up to its neck, to squeeze. Easy. Just press.

The bird yanked its head round and jabbed its beak into the boy's hand, once, twice, three times, and then flew off to the far side of the loft and stood still.

In his anger Rob didn't notice the pain. He felt foolish, beaten by a bird. Without thinking, he wiped the blood from his hand on to his shorts, along with the pigeon mess and sweat, and lunged at the bird many yards away.

For three paces he landed luckily on the beams, but luck ran out at the fourth stride, his foot cracked through the flimsy plywood and his left foot followed, despite his attempt to wrench himself round. Splinters of plywood sliced into his skin, from knee to thigh. His right leg bent painfully under him.

The bird stood and watched him, now a much shorter, legless boy. A chicken that had wandered into the outhouse below, looked up in alarm and saw a bodyless leg hanging from the ceiling, and red stuff dripping from it. If the chicken had stayed a little longer, it would have seen the leg disappear upwards, at just about the same time that the pigeon saw the boy's body regain legs.

Rob gave the pigeon up. He knew he wouldn't kill it, even if he could reach it. He left the loft and the outhouse. He was leaving the farm when he suddenly saw a dark passageway at the end of the farmhouse, and hanging from the ceiling some dead rabbits and pigeons. So that was where all the others had gone. The pigeon left in the loft must have been a hero pigeon, then, the survivor of a massacre. This made Rob feel better. Rob gazed at the hanging birds with great longing.

The only thing he'd ever stolen was a packet of stamps from Woolworths, to try to match Tom's huge collection. He'd never stuck them in his album, or even showed them to Tom. But now, bleeding, stinging, scared and a failure, he didn't hesitate. Into the dark passageway, where cold hit his body, though sweat dripped into his eye as he reached up and cut down a plump bird with the scout knife he kept in his pocket. Then back to Pete's, appalled.

The other two boys were being heros up trees. Rob saw them from a distance and slowed right down. He felt a mess. Was a mess. Was guilty, coming back with a crime on the end of a piece of string. He didn't feel guilty about robbing the farmer, but about misleading Pete and Tom, who were asking him to join the close friendship of a gang. Would the others be able to tell? Rob fancied the dangling corpse would open its beak and squawk, 'This boy's a fraud! This boy's a failure!

Banish him! Punish him!'

His belly twisting with nervousness, he held the bird up high for the others to see. At least he felt proud of the bird's size. If his enemy in the loft was a hero, this one, though slain, was a giant. Rob's chest began to swell with pride, guilt forgotten.

'See? Here. One great pigeon, caught by me.'

Pete and Tom started laughing as though they'd never stop, but would just drop out of the tree, helpless with mirth.

'What's up?' Rob asked, annoyed.

'Can't you tell a pigeon from a pheasant? Don't you know anything? Where d'you pinch it from?'

He went home, burning, speechless. As he walked through the park that he knew so well, he saw all his old mates kicking a ball about, and he joined them. They were OK, his mates. Things seemed better. He burned no longer. He strolled into the clean little rooms of his home – happy rooms, even though his dad was shouting at his mum the words Rob had shouted at the pigeon.

It was all right in his house. One day he'd go for a wider world, with carpets and grand pianos and trees up which you could be a hero, but not yet.

'Robert, we've got work to do, me lad,' said his mum, keen to get away from her husband's nagging. 'There's some slugs to be killed. That's your job . . .'

ADRIAN BURKE

They Flee from Me

It took the old man longer than he had expected to lose his dog.

He parked the car on the seafront and let the dog out of the hatchback door.

'Out you get, old girl,' he said. She landed with a click of paws on the wet tarmac. He bent to fasten her lead. 'Just wait a minute, can't you? Wait a minute. *Wait!* For goodness' sake - why can't you do as you're told for once?'

He let her off the lead. She dashed on ahead, tail up, nose down.

A sea mist started. The dog ran on. The man slowed down, then stopped quite still. He watched her at a litter bin, spilling over with food cartons and drink tins. But he did not yell at her. Instead he turned and walked away. When he got to his car he went to the back first, shook his head and then drove off.

She soon tired of the rubbish. Something was wrong. She could not find him so she ran on; then she could, so she stopped at his feet. She jumped up his legs, scrabbling madly with her paws and nuzzling her nose into him.

'Get off, you bloody mongrel, you,' the stranger said. He pushed her away and walked on. She was confused. It was not him. It was just a man who happened to wear a blue jacket.

'Where is she then?' she called to her husband from the kitchen. 'Frank!' Where's my little Jenny? Frank?'

He went in the bedroom and hung up his coat to dry. His wife followed him. The handle of the dog's lead swung from his fingers like a noose.

'Frank, where is she?'

'I got rid of her, duck.'

He let the lead fall to the carpet.

'You've done what, Frank?' his wife asked, stooping auto-matically to pick up the lead and hang it up tidily.

'I've got rid of her. It's no good. She's getting old. I must take a tablet.'

She found him in the lounge. He popped two green tablets into his mouth.

'Frank. How could you?'

'It was for her own good in the long run, pet.'

'You took her to the vet's, didn't you? My poor little Jenny. I knew you would one of these days.'

'But love,' her husband said, 'she was getting so poorly that even her walk up to get the papers did her in for the rest of the day. You said so yourself.'

'Well, I know but you didn't have to have her put down. Without even discussing it. How could you, Frank? To think that two hours ago she was curled up in her basket in the kitchen – and now she's . . .'

'Well, there you are,' he said, 'that's another point. A kitchen's no place for a dog. Particularly a sick one. It's not hygienic. It's unhealthy. The doctor wouldn't approve.'

'Well, he told me that people who keep pets live longer.'

'Rubbish!' her husband snorted.

'She kept you going.'

'As if!'

'She gave you an interest. A purpose. A reason for getting out of bed in the morning. Something to do now you're retired.'

'She was just a dog for heaven's sake.'

'Just a dog, Frank. She was much more than that. You had no right.'

'It was the kindest thing to do. We've been through this all before. She couldn't help herself. I wanted to spare her the pain of growing old. So I did something about it. We're better off without her. We're free now. To do as we please.'

'I bet our kids say that about us!' his wife retorted.

'We can go abroad now. You'd like that wouldn't you?'

'Oh, Frank. You've turned into a liar and a bully in your old age. I won't listen to you any more.'

He looked for his pipe on the mantelpiece.

'It was time we did something about her. Where's my pipe?'

'I threw it out. Not like that. Not without even discussing it. Poor little thing.'

'Look,' said Frank, 'she's getting old. Her eyesight's going. So's her heart. She's starting to smell. She finds it even harder to walk now and you know she's getting to be incontinent. She's getting to be no use to man nor beast.'

'Like you,' his wife said.

There was a knock at the door. A young policeman stood in the porch with the dog.

'Oh,' she said. 'You'd better come in. My husband's in the lounge.'

Released, the dog leapt through the doorway and fussed over her master. He took off his glasses and stooped over the cringing, trembling animal. Her fur was damp and smelled of dog.

'Now look here,' the policeman was saying. 'This is the fourth time this month that this dog has been found out loose and returned to you. It makes me cross. You old folk aren't fit to have pets in my opinion. Do you hear me?'

But the old man was not listening. He had started to stroke her now, with his hands, as if he had to relearn a once lost rhythm.

Keep Quite Still!

He was lying there, minding his own business, head propped on an air-filled cushion. The sea lapped round him. His fingers trailed in the sand, and the water crept in between his fingers and up into his armpit, warm and ticklish. This was his favourite place. There was not a great difference between low and high tide here, he had learned. He had worked out the best place by lying on the beach each day, moving a little each time. Now he had it just right. The sea would just wash round him and warm him and then, like a brief but unhurried visitor, be gone again. Unless there was a storm, of course. But today there would be no storm, only a hazy sky and the rhythmic wsh, wsh, wsh of very small waves breaking very close by.

A stone or a shell nudged his outstretched fingers. He let it. That was part of the game. You never moved. On the second day he had lain here, his mother came worrying up to him, disturbing the perfect peace. He would get sunburnt, or worse, sunstroke, she said. To be stroked by the sun sounded nice, but so as not to upset her he wore a floppy white hat which shaded most of his face. His skin was already brown, but he smoothed in some oil each morning just in case. The shell or seaweed or whatever it was, tickled strangely. Perhaps there was a crab crawling over his hand. He had long ago stopped worrying about such things hurting him. If he did not move suddenly, it would not do anything. The only things he did not like were jellyfish and sea urchins and they would not come clambering over his hands.

There must be something there, he thought, and curiosity overcame him. He edged his head up just a fraction and peered under the brim of the sunhat. Just as he did so, he felt a sharp pain in his middle finger, between the knuckle and the joint. He would have jerked it away if his eyes had not

63

focussed on the cause at just the same moment. The cause of
the pin prick was – well, something very much like a pin, a
short pin sticking into his finger. Attached to the pin was a
piece of string and attached to the string was a boat.

A boat about three centimetres long was tied up in the
sheltered cove between his first and middle fingers. Several
figures a centimetre high were just then clambering out onto
his hand, joining the one who had waded ashore and driven
in the pin.

He tried not to shout or to jump or to do anything
sudden. He tried to content himself with saying under his
breath over and over, 'Good grief, it can't be true; good
grief, it can't be true.' For a moment he thought, 'My
mother's right. I've got a touch of the sun. I'm seeing things.
'I'm delirious. I shall be seeing palm trees in the desert next.'

But no. The images were clear enough. And now he could
hear high-pitched sounds which he knew were voices. Tiny
voices from tiny people. 'Why here?' he thought, 'when
there's the whole of the beach, the smooth soft beach?' Then
he realised that to a small boat such as this the wide open
beach would provide little shelter. His arms, his fingers,
were ideal havens.

There were six of them and they walked in a little procession up across his wrist and along his lower arm. The
tickling had stopped. The feeling was a pleasant regular
touch, much as you would get if you walked your own
fingers up your arm. Stretched out as he was, it was hard to
focus properly – but he could make out blue shirts and white
trousers and dark hair, some of it long. Where were they
going?

The thought of them walking over his face made him
wince. Maybe they would use his ear as a cave. Or camp on
his forehead in the shade, driving in lots of little pegs to
hold up their tent. Perhaps they would light a fire! He
imagined a campfire in his eye and almost jumped up there
and then, scattering them over the sand and the sea. But no.
He resisted. Nothing bad had happened yet. If anything did
happen he could pick them off as easily as ants – more
easily, in fact.

Now they were at the top of his arm and approaching his shoulder. They stopped and seemed to be talking and pointing. 'They don't know which way to explore,' he thought 'head or body. Body is easier, nice and flat and open . . . but head is more interesting. Depends what they're looking for.' There was something in his mind that made him look more closely at the figures . . . 'Ahh,' he thought . . . 'of course. Now, I *really must* keep very still.'

The party had split into two groups. One seemed to stay put on his shoulder, the other group clambering awkwardly up the side of his chin. He could hardly make out anything by sight now, but the touch of their feet made their progress very clear. He closed his eyes. He did not want to take any risks. They paused on his cheek and then almost immediately headed for his nose. He held his breath. Into his right nostril went one or two, maybe three of them.

He had an almost irresistible urge to sneeze but he willed his body to stay still. He heard the high birdlike sound of voices. The probing and poking inside his nose was becoming painful. He would have to do something. He needed to breathe. Then the foraging and probing stopped. The feet stood around on his upper lip. He imagined them looking out to sea. There was a sound – almost like singing – perhaps cheering. Then, hurrying, the figures made their way back down the side of his face, back to his shoulder and all six of them began their procession towards the harbour of his hand.

In a few minutes they had reached the boat. The pin was pulled out and, with a final tickle, they were gone. He felt a strange mixture of disappointment and relief. His eyes now safely open, he could see the boat pulling away into the breakers. Then a small sail was hoisted and the vessel gathered speed. He kept his eyes on it for as long as he could. Even after it had disappeared from sight he lay unmoving for a long time.

It was only when he heard his mother's voice calling him that he stirred. He sat up. He looked at the small pin prick on his finger and then, carefully placing his hand underneath, blew sharply through both nostrils. A small hard object fell into his hand. It was a box. A tiny, tiny box with a minute lid. He prised it open with his fingernail and smiled with delight at the sparkling pinhead treasures inside.

ROGER BURFORD-MASON
Moving

Mum keeps cracking on about how much she likes this house more than the last one. I don't blame her, but I don't.

Mind, it was fun moving. Everywhere was upside down, the furniture was piled up, and when it was loaded up you couldn't believe you could get all our house into one removal lorry.

But what was best, was going through all the drawers and cupboards when we were clearing them out, and finding things none of us ever knew were there, like Dad's old ice skates – he never let on he'd ever skated before – and an old silk sunshade Mum had when she was a girl, before she came to England. All sorts of unexpected things. It was like finding out about yourself. That's one good reason why I don't like this new house. There aren't enough cupboards. In the other house there were lots; you could play hide and seek in them, or sit quietly out of Mum's way when she was in one of her moods. We used to let on we'd seen mice in them and then she'd go and drag everything out and set a trap with a bit of bread or bacon rind. Then in a few days she'd go back in to see if she'd caught anything. One time she did – a tiny little mouse that the trap had almost cut in two when it sprang shut, but she was so upset that she had Will and me take it up to the apple trees and bury it. She never set a trap after that, and when we said we'd seen a mouse in the cupboard she used to say, 'Well let the little devil stay there then!' So we stopped teasing her about it.

One time Mum got *really* angry and I wanted to go and hide in the cupboard like I usually did, but I was so frightened that I just stayed where I was, sat on the stool by the fire.

It was January and I'd been sliding on the pond and snowballing, and some of us had built a snow fort. Anyway, it got dark, but we didn't notice because we were enjoying ourselves, and then suddenly I saw Mum tramping across the field towards us and I could tell she was angry, just by the way she was walking. I stood and waited for her and she came straight up to me and fetched me such a clout round the head that I fell over and started to cry. She dragged me up and hurried me home, raging about it being dark and hadn't I got any thought for her getting worried and what sort of a home would people think I came from, out larking all night?

When we got home she said for two pins she wouldn't let me have any tea, but I knew she was calming down because she started to go round singing, and soon she was in a good mood again. I was frozen through, and wet, so I sat in the corner on the stool by the fire and ate the bread and jam she brought me and drank the tea, and listened to the wind sucking and blowing in the chimney.

She said I wasn't to go sliding on the pond again, but now she was calm and worried, not angry and worried, and to tell the truth I could see it from her point of view. She was right. Even if it froze every day for a week, the river ran quickly and there was no way of being sure that the ice would set really hard. She said she remembered a boy drowning years ago when he fell through ice on the pond. It wasn't a nice way to go. I looked up at her and there were tears in her eyes, so I said I wouldn't do it again and she smiled, and that was the truth, because I never did go sliding on the pond again.

Anyway, after we'd had our tea and she'd cleared away and washed up, she came and sat in her chair on the other side of the fireplace. She had her knitting on the go and one of her women's magazines, and I was watching the telly. All the others were out except Terry, and he was in bed because he was the baby, so there were just the two of us and it was nice and cosy.

We'd been sitting there for a while when the back door banged shut. Mum said that it was Dad, which was pretty obvious really, but she usually said obvious things like that. Dad called out that it was him and Mum called back that his tea was in the oven, but she didn't get up to see to it.

Then Dad came in. Well, that's not quite true. He didn't come in, he just seemed to fill up the doorway and stand there, neither in nor out of the door. Behind him there was a young woman. I guessed Mum couldn't see her from where she was sitting, but I could from my corner. He looked a bit strangely at Mum and tried to say something but whatever it was, it came out in a stutter you couldn't make sense of. For a moment he stood there looking into the room with a kind of false smile on his face, then he moved so Mum could see the young woman.

Mum stared at her for a moment and her jaw worked as if she was going to say something. Then she got up and pushed past them into the hall. Dad pushed the woman into the room and told her to sit down and then he went after Mum, and I could hear him calling after her up the stairs.

The woman came into the room and stood for a moment as if she didn't know what to do, smiling a bright sort of a smile that you knew she was forcing herself to put on. She was going to sit down in Mum's chair but I told her, so she quickly went over to the mantelpiece and looked at the ornaments. She asked me my name and how old I was and I told her, but she wasn't really listening, she was watching the door. I sat and stared at her.

She was younger than Mum but older than our Judy. Judy worked in the newspaper office and was getting engaged, so she was probably about twenty-three. She had lots of black hair and bright red lips, and she was wearing a kind of knitted suit and big padded coat.

I wondered who she was and what she was doing coming home from the match with Dad and I was just going to ask her when we heard Mum explode with a shout.

'Liar!' she cried. 'Liar! Liar! Liar!'

You could hear her as clear as anything, and Dad shouting at Mum, but I couldn't understand what it was he was saying. I looked at the woman. She was straining forward to catch what was going on and biting her bottom lip, and there were tears starting in her eyes. She gripped the edge of the mantelpiece for a moment and her knuckles were white with tension, and then she leaned forward and put her forehead down against it and stood like that as the noise from outside raged backwards and forwards – Mum's shrill screaming,

Dad's voice deeper, slower, but just as angry.

Suddenly Mum burst into the room and crossed to the fireplace. Before Dad or the woman could say or do anything, she fetched the woman a belt across the side of her head and the woman staggered. Dad leapt forward and caught Mum's hands and made her sit down in her chair, although she shouted and struggled for a moment until it was clear he was too strong for her. The woman sat down at the table, stroking the side of her face where Mum had caught her. It was already good and red and she was crying softly. She swore at Mum and Mum swore and shouted back at her, while Dad tried to get them to be quiet. He kept saying, 'Let's be more adult about this,' but it was a few moments before the noise subsided and the two of them stopped yelling.

Mum was quiet for some time, staring blankly at the wall, rocking backwards and forwards gently in her chair, and crying. Dad put his hand on her shoulder but it didn't do anything so after a moment he took it away again. The other woman just sat and stared at her hands.

After a while Mum stopped rocking and sat perfectly still.

'Take her away from my house, Frank,' she said in a flat, small voice.

Dad looked intently at her for a moment but she looked past him at the wall. He stood uncertainly for a moment and then went round the table and took the young woman by the arm and led her out. As he closed the door behind them, Mum suddenly picked the teapot up off the table and shied it at them, but it broke against the door and fell in a mess of pieces and teabags onto the floor, leaving a long, wet stain down the green paintwork.

Mum stood by the table for a long time, staring at the table cloth while full, heavy teardrops fell down her cheeks onto the cloth. No one had paid the slightest attention to me the whole time, but after a while she came over and knelt in front of me and put her arms round me, as if it had been me that was crying. I hugged her and tried to think of something to say, but nothing came, so we sat there without speaking. Eventually she straightened up and began picking up the pieces of the teapot and clearing up the mess. I asked her where Dad and the woman had gone but she just shook her head and went out into the kitchen and I heard her throw the pieces in the bin.

When the others came in, she talked about it to them for a long time and Will said it was a bloody good job and that we'd be OK, he'd see to that. Judy saw me off to bed but wouldn't answer any of my questions, and when I was tucked up, she hurried downstairs again without reading me a story like she usually did. I went to sleep and dreamed of Dad, skating on the pond, and Mum shouting at him to be careful.

It was never the same after that. Mum hardly ever played with us, and she got cross very easily. Will jacked in his job training to be an accountant and got a different job where he could earn more money and didn't have to study at nights. And when people started talking about Dad, Mum or Judy or Will would shut them up straight away. Me, I played more and more by myself in the garden, or went on long hikes in the woods, and hardly ever had friends home to play like before, but I quite liked it like that. I've always enjoyed my own company.

Then, one evening, Mum said we were going to move. She'd got another house quite a distance away, and a job, and we were going to start a new life. We all got excited and fired questions at her until she hushed us all and gave us the details.

After that, time seemed to fly, until one morning we all got up early and began sorting things out and packing the china and glass in newspaper, and clearing out shelves and cupboards and taking up carpets and stacking furniture. By mid-afternoon it was all loaded into the removal van and we were ready to go but there was no sign of Mum.

The driver and Will went round the outside of the house to see if she was out in the shed or down the garden, but I went back inside because I knew she'd be having a last look round.

She was in the kitchen, sitting on the floor. I stood in the door looking at her, not knowing what to say, and then I saw that she was holding a bit of the old brown teapot in her lap and the tears were washing down her cheeks and dropping onto her hands. She looked up at me and tried to smile, and after a moment wiped her eyes on her sleeve and held out her hand for me to help her up. She stood and smoothed down her dress, and as we were going out of the kitchen she threw the piece of crockery into the sink.

RICHARD BENNETT
Lucy and the Dolphins

If you think you are thick, don't worry about it. It doesn't really matter. What matters is that you are happy. If you are brainy like me, it's too much like hard work. Lots of brainy kids like me aren't happy because they always want to be perfect. They always want to get ten out of ten. They always want to get As.

I'm brilliant at everything. It makes me sick. I'm the one all the other kids call 'swot', 'licker', 'creep' and 'Goody Two-Shoes'.

Kids without pens or pencils come to me . . . 'Can I borrow your black pen, Lucy?' 'Can I borrow your crayons, Lucy?' 'Can I borrow your ruler, Lucy?'

They come to me because they know I will always have everything. But I haven't got everything. I'm not happy. I'm not happy at all.

'Lucy Jones'; you see how neat and tidy the name sounds? Everything I do, everything I touch, turns out well. I can do things without even trying. It's just the way I am, tidy, neat and good.

At home my mum and dad are very straight, very clever and very proud. My dad works in a bank. My mum works for the Church. Our house is so perfect. I daren't leave a cup on the floor or a crumb on the carpet. My mum would kill me. I have to tidy my room every day before I go to school. I have to clean my shoes and pack my bag the night before. My packed lunch is made three weeks before I need it and frozen. We have a freezer full of packed lunches, marked 'Mum', 'Dad' and 'Lucy'.

My dad works on the house every weekend; even when it's raining or temperatures are freezing, my dad will paint the house or pick up dead leaves off the lawn. He doesn't like football; he'd rather pick up dead leaves. I can't talk to Mum or Dad about the way I feel. I'm not happy.

So, I'm going to play a game. I'm going to play with a two pence piece. I'm going to be the servant of the coin. The coin rather than other people decides what I do for a while. I'm going to see what it is like being somebody different. *The coin* decides what I do.

It works like this. I set myself a task and I toss *the coin*. So let's say I decide the task is to tidy my bedroom. The coin decides, heads for yes, tails for no. I am the servant of *the coin*.

Today the task is to take the wrong packed lunch. The coin said *heads . . . Yes.* So I took my dad's packed lunch. I felt really bad about it because I knew it would cause a stir. But in a way it was exciting.

My dad got home in the evening. He looked as though the world was going to end. He hadn't eaten the sandwiches. His normal day was knocked sideways. He could not cope. He went to bed early and slept. He was in a state of shock. I had made a mistake for the first time in my life and my dad couldn't believe it. He couldn't talk to me about it. He never will.

The coin said *heads . . . Yes* to not taking any pens or pencils to school the next day.

I could not do any work without borrowing a pen from somebody else. I felt really bad about going to school with nothing to write with. Some kids in my class do that everyday. In the English lesson that morning loads of kids couldn't do their work because I had forgotten my pencil case. Even Mr Webb, our English teacher, couldn't work because he usually borrowed a pen from me too! The whole lesson came to a stop and we ended up watching a video. Mr Webb wondered if I was ill because I'd forgotten my pencil case.

The coin said tails . . . *no* to missing afternoon registration so I went.

The coin said *tails . . . no* to missing PE. So I played basketball. As usual I ran rings around the boys who always think they are playing rugby.

The coin said *heads . . . Yes* to not doing any homework that night. My mum and dad couldn't believe I didn't have any homework. Sometimes I did extra homework on a Saturday night. Here I was on a Tuesday without any work whatsoever. I watched television. I saw the News three times! I couldn't believe how sad all the news could be.

The next day I went into school and told all the teachers that I hadn't done my homework. I couldn't believe the answers I got . . . Mr Bell, my Maths teacher, said, 'It's OK, Lucy'. Mrs Thomas, my Physics teacher, said, 'Copy it up, Lucy'. Mr Webb, my English teacher, said, 'It's OK, Lucy. I have problems with my pens, too.' Not one of those teachers had a go at me for not doing my homework. Not one spoke to my Year Head about it. Even they think I am perfect. Even they think I am happy, but I'm not.

The coin said *heads* . . . *yes* to sorting out Mr Bell, my Maths teacher. In class he always comes and helps me when I don't need help. The worst thing about him is he smells. He smells of stale beer and chicken curry. He leans over me and breathes and leers. It's horrible.

I sprayed Mr Bell with really sweet-smelling aftershave, gave him a mint and then put on a gas mask. I think he took the hint.

Mr Bell told me to get out of his class. At least that's what I think he said – I couldn't really hear him under the gas mask. It's the first time I've ever been sent out of a class.

Mr Bell couldn't really tell me off because in the back of his mind he knows that I am right. He is a smelly teacher. He is a pervert.

All I'm doing is playing a game. I'm doing nothing that really pleases me, nothing that makes me really happy inside. I'm only bugging other people by being a rebel. A rebel without a cause. I need some direction. I feel like a dolphin stuck in a small aquarium.

The coin had dropped! That's it! There are two dolphins in our local aquarium. I have seen them. They are not happy either. They lack direction too. They swim around the pool all day looking for a place to go, looking for a direction. They want to get out into the open sea and swim anywhere, anytime. Their lives need to be happy, like me they want to be free. They want to be themselves.

The dolphins are called 'Splish' and 'Splosh'. I ask you,

who would call them that? The younger kids in our town love them. The tourists love them. 'Splish' and 'Splosh' have a life of sadness. They have a life that is short because all they do is swim around the small pool. All they do is perform for us humans. If they were out in the sea, at least they could be happy and swim anywhere. At least they could be themselves and have a direction.

The coin said *heads* . . . *yes* to freeing those two dolphins. Even if the coin had said *tails* . . . *no*, I'd have done it. I'd have tried to let them go free. But how am I going to do it?

The feeling I get from just thinking about freeing those dolphins makes me giggle. It even makes me laugh out loud, that's how happy it makes me. That feeling inside is good. Lucy Jones is going to be happy. But how am I going to do it?

I went to look at the dolphins. I paid £2.50 to get into the Bude Aquarium. I watched Splish and Splosh perform. They had to do things like go through a hoop, head a ball, play a trumpet and swim backwards. All the time I thought to myself, I know how you feel, I perform because somebody tells me what to do. But inside I want to do something, too. They must dream of the open sea.

The Bude Aquarium is right next to the sea. It is made of concrete. It is surrounded by a ten foot high fence. So how on earth am I going to free those dolphins? How does a 14-year-old schoolgirl free two dolphins? I'm supposed to be perfect. I can't think of anything. Maybe *the coin* can help.

The coin said *tails* . . . *no* to breaking down a wall of concrete!
The coin said *tails* . . . *no* to using a crane!
The coin said *heads* . . . *yes* to chatting up the dolphin keeper!
Oh my God!

The dolphin keeper's name is John Hay. He is tall, blond and about 25 years old. I have a task to chat him up and find out about the dolphins.

I went again to the Bude Aquarium. I payed £2.50 and when the show was over I went to talk to John Hay. He answered all my questions: 'Where have the dolphins come from?' 'How old are they?' 'Would they survive the open sea?' 'Does the aquarium have a link to the open sea?' 'Do you think they are happy?'

He told me the dolphins only live up to half their normal length of life because they are so unhappy in the pools. He looked at me and I knew, for some reason I just knew, that he was going to help me. The pool has a link to the sea. It has a grate behind a trap door. It is at the side of the pool. The keys to the trap door are kept by John Hay. I didn't have to say a word but John Hay knows, he knows what I am thinking.

John Hay started to laugh and I laughed with him. We both felt the same way. We both knew what we were about to do was going to make us happy.

The Bude Aquarium was empty of people, the sun was going down and we jumped fully clothed into the pool. John Hay unlocked the trap door. I pulled it open and the grate easily came away too. Splish and splosh swam towards us and looked at the sea . . . in a moment they were gone. No looking back.

In a moment I felt really happy. The next day John Hay lost his job. But it didn't matter – he was happy, too. He told me he had wanted to free those dolphins from the time he first saw them. He just needed a bit of a push. *The coin* had a lot to answer for.

So what about me? Well, somehow by letting those dolphins go it helped me too. I stopped playing *the coin*. I started making my own choices. And, I started to be myself and, therefore, be happier.

It was a week later. My dad showed me the newspaper headline:

Dolphins found washed up on Bude sands.

I cried my eyes out. For a small time in their lives they had known freedom. I have the chance to be free for the rest of my life.

FAY WELDON

You Never Know What You've Got Till It's Gone

It was hard to believe that such a terrible thing could happen on such a beautiful day. But happen it had. The early sun, for once, shone warm and bright in the square where the children of Cruxton waited for the school bus, and the daffodils had chosen that morning to open all along the village street, but all Annie wanted to do was cry.

Terrible things happened, of course they did, but not in Cruxton. Bombs went off, aircraft crashed, ferries sunk, but somewhere else. Even in Cruxton some people had a hard time – fell ill, went to prison, got divorced. But whoever expected anything awful to happen in their own home?

'Where's Alan?' asked Annie's best friend, Rose. 'Is he ill?' It was good of Rose to ask. Alan usually tagged along behind Annie, and embarrassed everyone. No one sat next to him. He was the only pupil on the bus who went to Summerkind Boys. Everyone else went to Stopland Girls. 'Yes', said Annie, who hardly ever lied. The truth of the matter was that when she'd gone to wake her young brother up that morning (he slept like a fat white slug – she'd tell him so – and right through the alarm) Alan just hadn't been in his bed. It hadn't ever been slept in. A vanished brother was hard to take in. Annie had done all kinds of silly things like looking for him under the sofa, behind doors. All no good.

'Run away?' she'd heard her mother half-crying, half-shrieking on the phone to the police. 'Boys of ten don't run away for no reason!' 'Why should he run away?'

'You never know what you've got till it's gone,' Annie said now to Rose, who said, 'What?' and then the schoolbus veered around the corner towards them in its usual cloud of fumes, and Rose said,'Where are you going?' because all of a sudden Annie took to her heels, her yellow and pink trendy rucksack bouncing on her back. 'You'll get into awful trouble!' Rose yelled after her, but Annie didn't care. The trouble had arrived already. It was all around.

The Gallows Haunting

It was cold that night; a bitterly unwelcome cold that froze the hair to your face in the driving wind. I was a long way from home.

It was my Christmas visit to my father. I didn't see him much these days, since he'd become so gloomy and bad tempered. I think he missed my mother, wished he'd been better to her, now; but she'd left him, and gone with someone else to another place. Stephen and I shared a flat, we two brothers, in the city. We both had jobs, we were young, and we had hope, unlike my father. Stephen didn't visit at all.

'Miserable old man,' Stephen used to say. 'Let him rot in his grotty little seaside flat, I don't care.'

But I felt bound to go. Something in that cheerless place of his drew me there – perhaps it was my own guilt, for I hadn't been very nice to him either in those last few years.

'Why don't you get out more, Dad?' I said to him that evening – the last time I was ever to see him, as things turned out.

'Get out? Get out?' he muttered, turning the gas fire down to a low, blue flame. I shivered and put my coat around me. The place was draughty, full of creakings and sighing noises.

'Yes, out,' I said firmly and loudly. 'You know, enjoy yourself.' My father looked up.

'Enjoy myself? Huh! Little you know, little you know about what it is to be old.'

'You're not old,' I said, flinching as the lights flickered, plunging us into darkness for a few seconds. It was the storm, of course. 'You're not old,' I continued, 'and you shouldn't mope about like this. You should have more friends.'

'Friends!' My father spat into the gas fire, making it hiss and flare up again. 'What good are friends? And wives? And children? They only desert you in the end.'

'Friends are company.' I was determined to make my point. The lights blacked out again, and a sound came from behind the wall of the shabby room. It sounded like no wind I'd ever heard – but then, you got some strange effects on this coast.

'Company.' My father looked up, a little smile on his face. 'Oh, if it's that you're worried about – I have company.'

'You do?' I blinked as the lights came on again.

'Oh yes. I have *company* all right.' He spoke with a kind of sarcasm. 'Every night.'

Now I was really startled. In all of my visits I had never seen another mug or cup around, or any sign of a visitor.

'I've never met another human soul here,' I said. 'What are you talking about?'

My father chuckled – a dry, hard, unpleasant sound. 'That's the point,' he said. 'You won't see another human soul. I have company of quite a different kind.'

I jumped up out of my chair. This was really getting too much. I shoved my arms rapidly into my sleeves as the lights flicked on and off, and a brilliant jag of lightning lit up the room.

'Oh, you're going now, are you?' My father laughed again. 'So you're not staying to meet my friends – the friends you keep telling me I should have?'

'Look, Dad, it's late,' I said. 'The roads are bad.'

I paused, looked down at him hunched in his chair. He was just an old man, lonely, with not enough to occupy his time.

I stood by the door, not really wanting to leave him, but knowing I must get back. The snow would be drifting and I didn't fancy getting stuck out in these parts. My father said nothing, but turned away from me and huddled back into his old armchair. The room seemed very dim.

'You'll be all right?' I said.

He did not reply, but shrugged his shoulders; so I left him.

Outside, the wind forced the door from my hand and tore at my coat and scarf. I had forgotten how wild this coast could be. I looked around me as I struggled to the roadway outside. It was a shock to see how much snow had fallen; several inches on the hedges, and drifting heavily. My car was already covered in a thick layer of the stuff.

Cursing, I scraped the snow off my windscreen and opened the door. Freezing air rushed into the car. I put the key in the ignition, with clumsy fingers. Turned it. Nothing! Just a click. Then I remembered. Damn it! I'd had trouble with the starter motor earlier in the week. Frantically, I turned the key, switched off, turned again, and again, but it was no use. The thing was dead.

'Dad!' I yelled from the front door. 'Come and give us a push start will you? Car won't go.'

There was no reply, and I went into the house. I noticed that all the passage lights were off again; the place was in total darkness. I groped my way to my father's sitting room.

I could just see my father standing near his mantelpiece, straining my eyes in the darkness – and then I got the shock of my life. For his face seemed lit up, as if from within, and he was grinning. His eyes glittered at me in triumph.

'You'll have to stay now,' he sneered. 'You'll stay the night.'

'Dad?' I gulped. I suddenly felt as if someone were trying to choke me. 'Dad, come and give me a push off. Please!'

'Oh, no,' said my father, grinning more widely. 'Not at my age, and with my heart, in this weather. It would probably kill me!'

'Haven't you got a light?' I said, desperately. 'For God's sake, Dad – we can't sit like this. And it's so bloody cold.'

My father turned to a cupboard, and brought out some candles. He placed the candles about the room, and they cast their shadows everywhere. He sat down in the chair again, and I sat opposite him. For a while, we sat like that, not speaking, until I could not stand it any longer.

'Dad,' I said, 'perhaps I could sleep on the settee. Have you a blanket or something? I'm tired and it's freezing in here.'

For a moment, he did not answer, that strange expression on his face. Then, he seemed to rouse himself.

'You're not going to go to sleep, and miss my visitors? There is one I think you'd – particularly like to meet.'

'Oh, Dad, for goodness' sake – not that nonsense again! Look, I'll have to get up early tomorrow and see what I can do about the car. Where are the blankets? And how about a cup of tea?'

He pointed to an old chest, but waved away the cup of tea I offered, so I drank it myself. I lay down on the hard sofa and covered myself with the thin quilt I had dug out. I kept my coat and all my clothes on, as the temperature was dropping steadily to an unnatural coldness, a cold that started in the bones and spread outwards to my whole body.

My father stayed in his chair, his head nodding, and then he would sit upright, a watching, listening expression on his face. I thought he would go to sleep in his own good time – and anyway, I was too dog-tired to care.

After about an hour of restless dozing, I fell sound asleep.

I don't know what time it was when I awoke, or how long I had slept, but it was still dark. My heart was thudding like a drum. Some noise had jerked me out of sleep. It was like the sound of timbers squealing, of rope binding – and then the dreadful throttling howl of a man being hanged by the neckbone until he was dead.

I sat up, clutching my covers to me. Where was my father? But the room was empty, and I was alone. Such stupid imagination! I told myself. This strange night in this terrible flat had got to me, given me a nightmare. I remembered that the flats were said to have been built on the site of an old, seafront gallows, where criminals were hung a century or more ago. This had no doubt come into my dreams, and woken me up. Such nonsense.

I lay down again, and slept. Again! That horrible sound! It echoed round the room, louder this time, and this time I swear I heard a terrible cursing – and then – oh, God, the noise of a bone breaking. My heart seemed to leap into my throat, and I wanted to cry out. The door of the room slowly opened.

It was my father! He carried in one hand a candle and in the other a bloody neckerchief. This he held in front of him like a banner, and behind him came other shadowy forms. I did not want to see more, and covered my sight, but my father jerked my head back by the hair so that I was forced to look.

'Here are my *friends*! he hissed. 'Now, you *shall* meet them!' He glared at me for a moment, and then turned to the first.

'Allow me to present my son,' he said, with a flourish of the red stained, stinking neckscarf, which made my stomach heave. 'Michael, pay your dues to my *very good friend*, Jem Burkin!'

My father clutched my hand, and held it out to the ghostly fist.

My terrified eyes could hardly look, but my father thrust the candle closer, and then I saw – Jem Burkin, victim of the hangman's noose. The fist made a sort of contact with my own hand, and it felt clammy, slippery and sharp, like a damp claw. I shivered violently, and my father laughed.

'Don't you like my Jem? Isn't he to your taste? Well let me tell you, he's a gentleman with a long pedigree in crime that makes you look pretty small!'

And as I stared at this ghostly man, with a mouth gaping in his swelling face, my father told me what had brought Burkin to his death in the year of 1767. He'd been a pirate, my father said, and had often sent others to their deaths. Burkin had suffered the double execution of a pirate. In those days, such convicts were left tied down on the cold seashore, whilst men kept watch for several high and low water marks to pass over them until they drowned. The worse their crimes, the more tides they had to endure, and by the look of him, Burkin had lain there for quite a while. After death by water, the corpse was hung upon the gallows as a warning . . .

Burkin passed from my sight, and there came another hollow form of a man: a triple murderer with reeking breath from two centuries ago, who had been, they said, most difficult to hang, having a neckbone as strong as an ox. In the end, the hangman had had to pull him down and finish off the job with an axe. The head lolled, the eyes bulged, the mouth twisted in an evil smile and the form drifted on, passing through me in its cold path, and out through the opposite wall.

And on it went, and on, this gruesome procession. Dickon James – hanged for thieving. Then came the highwaymen and footpads: Bill Towhill, still with his highwayman's pistols slung in his broad belt. Next, Walt Blackman – a double hanging that was, my father said, and I shuddered as I pictured the two bodies swinging by their necks in the wild winter storm.

I thought that it was the end, and began to pull myself together, thinking of escape. But there was one last thing – a swelling of greenish light in the room, and a sound like a thousand human souls screaming in Hell. My father whirled round, his eyes glittering in that strange way.

'Here she is!' he cried. 'Here you will meet the queen of my little company. For on this very spot the gallows stood, and I have the honour to guard it for my good friends! You, my son, have the privilege to meet the only woman hanged in this county in nearly two hundred years! Stand up, Michael, and meet her, my queen, my Katherine!'

Despite myself, I stood, on legs that felt as if they would not hold me. My father was mad, and I had better humour him, I told myself. But what I saw next drove all such thoughts from my head. Not even a madman could have imagined this!

A woman drifted slowly into the room, as if floating above the ground, like someone in a dream. Her long, beautiful red hair trailed almost to her feet, but it looked as if a rope or wild, tearing hands had hacked at it. As the figure turned its face to mine, I saw with a terrible shock that it was like looking in a mirror. Although this was a woman – and red haired where I am dark as the raven's wing – there was my own face. But great scars and scratches spoiled its beauty, the lips were bruised and cut, and the eyes drooped with tears. Out of that wide mouth, a copy of my own, came an endless wailing.

'I did not do it! For the love of our beloved Mary, mother of Jesus, tell them I am not guilty! I did not murder my child!'

The woman turned and came towards me. I could not move, for her eyes held me. Oh, my ghostly twin! A great sorrow dragged my heart almost from me, and I felt myself drawn into her.

And then she was gone from me. I felt a terrible pain, as if I was being pulled half in two, and I saw that my father was gone too, drifting after this sad young creature. He was like no earthly being now; he had gone beyond all things human.

The strange light followed him, and as I watched he seemed to take on the same ghostly form as the company he kept each night.

'Katherine!' his cry rang out. 'Wait for me! Wait for me!' The words echoed, the light began to fade, and suddenly there was darkness, and silence. The room grew a little warmer, and my father was gone. I knew that the shrunken form collapsed in the armchair was not him, but only his earthly body, and that his spirit had passed on.

Suddenly, the air seemed to choke me, and I had again that feeling of being strangled. I had to get away. Then I was stumbling, gasping, choking down the road, away from what I had seen. There, sitting behind the wheel of my car, was the form of Jem Burkin, grinning up at me! And I knew that they would find me, that they would come for me; and I did not want to join Katherine, who drew me to her with her beauty and her likeness to me. I had to get away, get away, get away . . .

It is cold tonight, this terrible night of 23rd December 1982; a bitter, unwelcome cold that freezes the hair against my face as I grope my way out of the street where my father lived. I can still hear the ghostly, mocking laughter of Jem Burkin and, even fainter, the sound I do not want to hear, the sobbing of a young, tragic woman with a face like my own. I stumble desperately along a path I am no longer sure of. I am a long, long way from home . . .

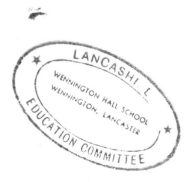

MALORIE BLACKMAN

Dad, Can I Come Home?

'Dad? Dad! It's Eve. How are you? What are you doing with yourself? Are you all right?'

'Eve? Eve darling, how are you? God, it's good to hear your voice. Where are you? Why can't I see you?'

Eve smiled happily. It was so good to hear if not see her dad again. Somehow it made the idea of returning home seem closer and more real. 'Dad, the screen of this videophone isn't working. And the fleet's just returned to Tdir-ah so the queues to use the phones are *ginormous*. It was use this phone or wait for another week to find a phone with a working screen.'

'No, no, it's enough just hearing your voice, bunny. Are you all right?'

'I'm fine, Dad.' Eve smiled again, stretching out a tentative arm to the blank screen before her. 'I've missed you so much. I just can't wait to get home.'

'So the reports are true? The war *is* finally over?'

'The war's over. The treaty was ratified three days ago. I should be home within the week, if the shuttle bus doesn't give up under the strain.'

'Bunny, that's great news. Wait till I tell Joe and Luke, and especially Morgan – eh!'

Eve's cheeks burned. 'Dad, stop teasing! Besides, Morgan is probably married with eight kids by now.'

'Of course he's not married. He's waiting for you. Mind you, if you told him that, he'd laugh in your face but it's the truth.'

'Is it, Dad? Is it really?'

''Course it is.'

'Listen Dad, I can't stay on the phone for much longer. There's a time limit on all comms to Earth until further notice. I . . . I wanted to ask you for a favour though.'

'Go ahead, bunny.'

Eve swallowed hard. This was it. 'You've met Janice my co-pilot. Did you like her?'

'Yes, of course I did.' Eve heard the surprise in her father's voice. She ran her dry tongue over her lips. 'It's just that . . . well, we were shot down over Zitunm . . .'

'*What*! You didn't tell me that . . . are you sure you're . . .'

'I'm fine,' Eve interrupted. 'But Janice . . . but Janice isn't, Dad. She was thrown clear but she went back to get me. She saved my life.'

'So what's the matter with her?'

'She . . . she was shot dragging me clear. Shot with a senso-blaster.'

'Oh, my God!'

'Exactly. She's lost an arm and both of her legs and her face is severely burnt – almost beyond recognition. And she's not eligible for artificial limbs because she broke the rules by going back for me. I know those artificial limbs aren't much use but at least they're better than the nothing she's going to get because of me.'

'Oh, my God. That poor, poor kid. And she was so pretty, so full of life. How's she taking it?'

'Not too well I think.'

Silence.

'Eve? What's the matter, bunny?'

'Sorry Dad, I was just thinking.' Eve forced herself to continue, 'Janice smiles a lot but I think that deep down she feels very scared, and very alone. She has no family, no one to go back to. So I said that she could stay with us.'

'Stay with us? For how long?'

'For good.'

Eve listened to the silence that filled the videophone booth. The unspoken plea reverberating through her mind deafened her.

'Eve darling, maybe Janice can stay for a day or two, or perhaps even a week, but no way can she live with us permanently.'

'Why not?'

'Eve, use your head. I'll always be grateful to Janice for saving your life. Always. But we have to face the facts. Janice is a cripple . . . she'll need a lot of time and attention. She'll require a lot of care, not to mention money. Our home is too small to have her here permanently and it would cost too much to adapt it.'

'But Dad, she saved my life. Couldn't we at least try? She wouldn't be too much trouble . . .'

'Yes, she would darling. Don't you think I'd love to say yes, but I can't. Maybe she could go into a hospital for the war wounded and we could visit her . . .'

'She'd hate that. *Please*, Dad . . .'

'I'm sorry, bunny, but the answer is no.'

'But I've already told her she could live with us.'

'Then you'll just have to untell her.'

'Couldn't we just try, Dad. *Please*, for me?'

'No, Eve. She saved your life and I'll always – *always* be grateful for that but she'd be too much of a burden.'

'Burden?' Eve whispered.

'I'm sorry Eve.'

Silence.

'Come on Eve. Let's not argue.I haven't spoken to you in over two years. Tell me all about . . .'

'I can't, Dad. My time's up now.'

'Already?'

''Fraid so. I'll see you soon. Bye, Dad. I love you.'

'I love you too bunny. I'm going to give you such a homecoming. And Eve, I'm sorry about Janice, but you do understand . . .?'

'I understand, Dad. Bye.'

'Bye, darling. See you soon.'

Eve switched off the videophone. She stared up at the peeling, dingy grey paint on the ceiling . . . and cried.

'Mr Walker, it's Janice Sonderguard here.'

'Janice? Well, hello Janice. How are you?'

'I'm all right Mr Walker.' Janice studied the image of Eve's father on the phone. He was just as she remembered, his hair grey at his temples but jet everywhere else. A neat, trim moustache and his skin the colour of oak, his body as sturdy as oak. And smiling eyes. A man you instinctively trusted. Solid, dependable. Only he was frowning now.

'Why, Janice, Eve told me that you'd lost an arm and your legs. Have the rules been relaxed? Have you received replacements after all?' Janice turned away from the screen, her lips a tight, bitter line. It didn't matter what the politicians and the diplomats said, the war wasn't over . . . not by *any* means.

'Congratulations. Eve must be so pleased for you.'

Janice turned back to the screen, staring at Mr Walker's broad grin.

'Mr Walker, *please.*' Janice hugged her arms around her body before dropping them to her sides. 'Mr Walker, please prepare yourself. I . . . I've got some bad news.'

'Eve,' Mr Walker said immediately. 'What's wrong? Has something happened to Eve?'

'Mr Walker, I don't know how to say this. Eve . . . Eve committed suicide this morning. I . . . I . . .' The man and woman stared at each other.

'Eve . . .?' Mr Walker whispered. 'She didn't . . . she wouldn't . . . What are you talking about?' The question was shouted at Janice.

'*Please*, Mr Walker, I'm telling you the truth. She's dead,' Janice shouted back. 'She's dead,' she whispered.

'But why? *Why?* I don't understand.' Janice jumped as Mr Walker punched the screen. 'Why are you doing this to me? Why?'

'Mr Walker, Eve spoke to you last night. Did you see her? What did she talk about?'

'What . . .?' Mr Walker shook his head slowly, utterly bewildered now, utterly lost. 'I can't . . . I . . . never saw her yesterday. The screen in the videophone booth wasn't working . . . She talked about you, she wanted you to stay with us.'

'Me?' Janice said slowly.

'She told me that you'd lost an arm and both legs.'

'Oh, I see,' Janice whispered.

'I don't understand,' Mr Walker pleaded.

'Eve left you a letter. Can I read it to you?'

Mr Walker nodded slowly.

Janice removed the letter from her overall pocket. There was sand in her throat, threatening to choke her as she began to read:

Sorry, Dad. I love you. You've explained everything to me very carefully and I think this is the best solution for everyone.

'What does that mean?' Mr Walker interrupted. 'Eve *can't* be dead . . . I don't believe it.'

'Mr Walker, let me show you Eve. She's . . . in the morgue. I can transmit the image to you.'

'I don't understand any of this . . .'

Janice keyed the necessary commands into the console beside the videophone and the morgue appeared without warning, filled to overflowing with row upon row of body capsules. Janice began to key in the commands to home in on the appropriate capsule.

'Mr Walker, did Eve tell you about our crash on Zitumn?'

'Yes, she told me how you saved her life.'

'I didn't save *her* life, Mr Walker,' Janice said quietly. 'It was the other way round. She came back for me . . .'

A new image filled the screen now. There in her capsule lay Eve Walker, Captain of the SAXICON ship, with no legs and only one arm and a badly scarred, almost unrecognisable face.

ROY SAMSON

Otherworld

My name's Cat. This may not be fancy, but I hate the trendy names we cats call one another these days. A Persian cat friend of mine once tried to rename me Artaxerxes, which is not a word I myself can say very easily, but she could purr it in a way that really turned me on. But no more of that. I've settled for Cat.

I think I'm special enough not to need a fancy name. I'm a tabby in the prime of life. I'm a well-balanced cat, even if I say so myself – I can walk along the narrowest of fences. I have many hobbies, among them chasing leaves, scratching my claws down furniture, crunching through the skulls of mice, licking my bottom and having plenty of juicy sniffs.

I also own quite a few things. My favourites are two tame elastic bands, a pigeon's feather, a male person and a ball of wool which I have patiently arranged into an artistic tangle. These are my favourites, but I get bored with them as I can always guess how they will behave. For instance, when I hook one paw inside the elastic band and pull it away from my front teeth, it always stretches in exactly the same way and then pings up into the air when it thinks I'm not ready. It seems to think it's really clever doing this. It's pathetic. Stretch, stretch, ping. Stretch, stretch, ping. Every time. I humour it and pretend I'm surprised, but it must be terrible to be so limited.

The only thing that I own that can surprise me is the male person. It was given me by a small white cat named Cat (I liked her no-nonsense attitude to life) who had grown tired of it. It interests me a good deal. I know persons can't really think, but sometimes it acts so cleverly it almost seems like a cat.

For instance, if one of those silly elastic bands springs up into the air, the person jumps after it and tosses it back to me in case it gets away. Of course it doesn't understand it's the elastic band's pathetic idea of a game, but it's still pretty clever. Cleverer than the elastic band, anyway.

I changed the person's name. The small white cat had called it Pinkie Short-Ears, but I thought that made it seem silly. I know a person's only a person, but it shouldn't be made to seem silly. 'Man' seemed too ugly a name for so cuddly an animal, and so I called him Tracey Z. Hammerstein the Second, which is special, beautiful and a name he can be proud of. I have a way with words, and was pleased with that name, though it's a bit of a mouthful when I have to call him to let him put down some Whiskas for me.

Tracey's pretty lucky with his owner. I think all creatures except birds and mice should be free, even elastic bands. So I've made him a person flap, and he can go in and out just as he chooses. My friends say I'm spoiling him. I know I'm taking a risk. I feel we should all be as natural as possible, and it really isn't natural to keep a person penned up in the house all the time.

I do worry about him being out during the day, as unpleasant things often happen to persons in the daylight, but I think the risk's got to be taken. If a gang of cats catches him and skins him, which is what's happening on our estate, then at least he will have a good life until then. It's the price of being free.

I try to get along with him, as one creature to another, not feeling above him. I never miaow down to him. We rub noses. I even shove my nose into his ear because he likes it, though what the Persian who calls me Artaxerxes would think, if she saw me doing it, I dread to think. She sways her hips in a very wonderful way, that Persian.

Sometimes I just gaze into Tracey's strange, rather frightening eyes, and wonder what goes on inside his head. What thoughts? Does he think at all? Or is he just a creature of habits?

Really a person is an alien creature. And here I am, sharing my house with one. Every so often something reminds me how strange Tracey's behaviour is. For example, he doesn't urinate sensibly. He doesn't spray it all around, to mark out his territory, but wastes it by peeing it all down the same hole. Every time. What sort of territory would he mark out for himself, I ask myself, if it wasn't for me? It's no wonder persons are still simple animals.

Yet I stick at it. I let him share all my floors, even though he sometimes smells unpleasant. He can't help it. I mean, I probably smell quite strange to him. You've got to allow for differences.

Even so, it's difficult to understand him. For a few weeks I tried to be as like him as I could, to see if he could respond. I tried urinating down the same hole that he uses, but as a result he behaved in an unhelpful way.

When my attempts to be like him failed, I tried it the other way round. I tried to teach him how to behave like me. When he started to eat on a table, which is a strange thing he always does, I would sweep his food on to the floor, so that he would eat it properly.

I clawed the sheets off his bed. It's unhealthy to sleep under rags (though I must say in most ways he's very clean. I've never had to put a litter box down for him).

He just didn't understand. His behaviour became more and more impossible. He shouted and screamed and waved his front paws around in a daft way.

One of the strangest things about him is that he mates just one at a time. I don't see the sense in that. The way we cats mate, with several at a time if possible, offers more chances. One night I caught him at it, in bed with just one female person. So I went round to several of my friends to borrow their pet female persons for a short while. Then I shut the female persons in the room with Tracey, so that he could do it properly. He seemed very cross.

In fact, he kicked me down the stairs. You'd be surprised how much strength they have in their back legs. I realised what a dangerous creature I was living with. He doesn't know how to be thankful. I'd taken him off another cat's paws, fed him, allowed him freedom, and tried to get to know him. And that's how he treated me. He was really a creature from another world.

So, very sadly, I've rung the vet, and am taking him to be

put down this evening. I shall be upset. He's a very pretty person. I'll lick his face when the vet sticks the needle into him.

ROGER BURFORD-MASON

Deeper and Deeper

There were two ways of reaching the swimming hole. You could walk along the railway track from the bridge on the back road leading out of the village, and where the railway crosses the river, you could tumble down the steep embankment through wild garlic and cinders; or you could trespass and go through the yard of the village school and the bottom of the headmistress's garden and then walk across the fields. The boy and girl took the second way.

They made their way in companionable silence for some distance under the shelter of the high thorn hedge. There were cattle in the field, grazing slowly or lying in the shade of the hedge, and they turned their heads with passive curiosity to follow them with their fly-plagued eyes until they passed by.

'Is it all thistles?' he called from several paces behind her as she passed through a gap in the hedge into the next field.

'Not entirely,' she said from the other side of the hedge. 'There's cowmuck too.'

He smiled and scrambled over the wire, catching her up in a few strides.

Something plopped into the ditch which crossed the field and they stood side by side watching its sleek head arrow through the scummy green water until it disappeared into a hole in the bank.

'Water-rat,' he said, almost to himself.

'What?' she said.

'You don't often see them out during the daytime,' he added. 'Come on.'

They crossed the ditch by the planks the tractors used as a bridge, and carried on diagonally across the field to the corner where the river flashed in the bright sun like a heliograph.

'I meant to bring us a drink,' she said after a moment. 'But I forgot. Sorry.'

They passed either side of a slurry of cowmuck and mud, raising a cloud of midges which buzzed in the air before settling in their wake.

'It's OK, I brought some,' the boy said

Wrapped in his towel there was a bottle of orange squash his mother had made up for them. It was still cold from the fridge against his thigh. She said nothing but turned to smile appreciatively.

They came to the river at last, placid at the corner of the field, where it ran under the high railway bridge into a deep pool which was locally called *Deeper and Deeper*. There was the stump of an old beech, long since cut down, to which barbed wire was nailed and then spread in strands across the river to prevent the cattle wandering into the deep pool. The hedge here was too tall and thick for them to penetrate it and so they climbed the wire. The girl went first, gingerly, while he steadied it, swinging her legs over the top strand and backing down on the other side. Once on firm ground she steadied the wire for him and he climbed it equally carefully, though with more practised ease.

The swimming hole was perhaps a mile from the village by both routes, but crossing the fields to it took longer because there were more distractions. You would certainly see pipits bobbing their black and white tails in wet mudholes beside the river, or dragonflies darting across the surface of the water, and if you were very lucky, you might see a kingfisher, none of which you would see taking the railway line.

He dropped to the ground and spread himself in the sun with the towel under his head. Above him arched the enormous blue of the sky, fringed incongruously with the top of the hedge which he could just see from where he lay. To his right the embankment rose abruptly to the parapet of the bridge and the single-track railway line. Beyond his feet, the green of the fields spread away in the direction they had just come.

'How long have you known about this place?' she said. She was sitting facing him with her knees encircled by her arms. Her question seemed strange until he remembered how recently she had moved to the village.

'I don't know,' he said after a moment. 'For ever, I think. Reincarnation. I knew about it in a former life.'

'Daft!' she said, waving a hand at the flies which were settling on her legs. 'Go on then, what were you before?'

'A bull,' he said. 'And an adder before that, with sharp fangs and gallons of poison.'

'Are there any?' She lay back beside him with her hands beneath her head.

'No,' he said, and then, 'Can't tell. I've never seen one, but that doesn't mean there aren't any.'

She didn't answer and he, looking sideways at her, saw that she had closed her eyes. Sun shone on the fine hairs on her arms. He rolled over onto his stomach and pulled a stem of grass.

'Do you believe in it?' he said, drawing the grass along her arm.

Almost immediately she flicked at it as if it were a fly and he whipped it away.

'What?' she said. 'Reincarnation? No.'

He teased her with the grass again.

'I do,' he said. 'That's why you see people who look like horses or dogs.'

She laughed. 'I'm dissolving,' she said. 'Coming in?'

She slipped out of her shorts and T-shirt and was already dressed in her costume underneath them.

'Last one in's a . . .'

But he was plunging past her towards the river. He raced her to the cattle gate across the river which was the second line of defence against wandering cattle, and crossed it ahead of her to the other side where the bank sloped into the deeper water. Together they pushed under the overhanging fronds of willow to reach a point on the bank where a tree trunk stood out over the water like a diving board. She edged a couple of feet along it and with a shout which echoed under the railway bridge, jumped out into the middle of the stream. He was a second behind her.

The water was cold and because it ran over gravel and stones at that point, as clear as tap water. They splashed and trawled and ducked and played, enjoying the coldness after the route march across the fields and the hot sun, until after ten or fifteen minutes she said she was going to get out. He dived under water and swam strongly towards her, surfacing right in front of her as she regained her feet in about three feet of water. His dripping face and hair was just inches from hers. For a moment she looked quizzically at him, and then quite deliberately leaned forward and kissed him on the nose. They looked at each other in surprise for a second and then, to cover his confusion, he did a backward dive, twisted under water, surfaced, and swam steadily upstream without looking back. Out of sight under the bridge, he trod water for a moment and then swam on, exchanging the gloom under the bridge for the bright sunlight on the open river. Once he was well out of sight he climbed out of the river and hauled himself onto the flat bank to sit in the sun.

He heard a train approaching and decided to watch it pass before going back to her. The two-coach diesel approached the bridge and he saw the bored faces at the window as they passed. How hot they would be, he thought, and how they would wish they could swim like him. For the benefit of the few who had noticed him and responded to his wave, he did a neat dive into the water and then allowed the slow current to carry him back towards the swimming hole, making an occasional stroke to keep himself in the midstream.

She was lying on the grass where they had lain before their swim, with the bottle of orange juice beside her.

'We should have kept it cool in the river,' she said as he approached over the cattle gate. She spoke naturally and smiled without a trace of the confusion and uncertainty he felt. 'Still, it tastes good,' she added, holding the bottle out to him.

He uncorked it and took a drink, automatically wiping the neck of the bottle before handing it back to her. She shook her head and put the bottle under a towel.

'There was a train,' he said lamely.

'I heard it,' she said. 'Was it a passenger?'

'Yes,' he replied settling down in the grass beside her. 'Almost empty.'

The sun was no longer overhead, although it was still hot and the sky still brilliantly clear. Somewhere he could hear crickets in the grass but when he propped himself up to try and locate them, they stopped their chittering.

'I wish we could stay here all the holidays,' she said at length.

'We can come here most days,' he said. 'Can't we?'

'Yes, I know that,' she said. 'But I mean not go back. Just stay he.e, like this, the river, the sun.'

'The orange squash wouldn't hold out,' he said, risking a joke because he didn't know how to answer her otherwise.

'There'd be the river,' she said.

'You couldn't drink it,' he said. 'You don't know where it's been.'

'We do know,' she said. 'It's come from up there, under the bridge.'

'Ah, but what's beyond the bridge?' he said. 'Might be cows peeing.'

'Or worse,' she said, 'Imagine!'

He stretched his hands out towards her and felt her fingers close on his. There was nothing in the sky except sky. He felt very happy.

'Listen. There. Four o'clock. Shouldn't we be getting back?'

She sat up as the first of four chimes carried distantly across the fields from the church clock.

'We don't have to if we don't want to,' he said, reaching for her hand again.

'No,' she agreed, and then after a moment, 'But we do.'

They dressed over their sun-dried swimming things without speaking and she put the bottle in her bag. In a moment they were picking their way back the way they had come.

'Are we going out together?'

'Are we?'

'I suppose we are really.'

Where the going was easy they sauntered, holding hands, and where they had to go in single file he went ahead and held his hand out behind him for her to hold.

Shortly they came to the barbed wire again but this time, in crossing it, she missed her footing, slipped, and tore her leg badly on the sharp barbs. He hurried over the wire after her, careless of his own safety, but without coming to any harm. In a moment he was kneeling beside her. The blood was running freely down her leg and discolouring her trainer. She mopped at the cuts with her handkerchief but in a second it too was sopping. He took his shirt off quickly and tore it into strips, ignoring her protests as she saw what he was doing. Hanging through the wire he trailed the strips of cloth in the river before strapping them clumsily round her cuts.

'Can you make it home, do you think?'

'Yes, of course I can,' she said, standing on her good leg. Her other leg was stained with thin rivulets of watery blood.

He put his arm under her shoulders and they set off again, she limping heavily and leaning on him for support. They made slow progress, but managed to get back to the village through the school garden and yard without being seen. Eventually they reached her house which was at the opposite end of the village to the little council estate where he lived.

'My God, what's happened child?' her mother exclaimed.

She explained what had happened while her mother fussed with disinfectant and sticking plasters. He stood awkwardly watching.

'I didn't know you'd gone swimming, dear,' she said. 'Are you sure it's clean?'

She explained to her mother how nice it had been and he was surprised to see a guarded look flit across the older woman's narrow face.

'Just the two of you, was there?' she said.

The girl blushed.

'I'd better be getting home,' he said, embarrassed. 'I'm sorry about . . .'

'It wasn't your fault,' she said quickly, with a glance at her mother. 'Thanks for a nice afternoon.'

'Shall I see you tomorrow, then?' he said at the door.

'She's . . .' her mother searched for the words. 'She'll be going out with me tomorrow. Visting her uncle.' She gave the boy a distant look. 'Another time perhaps.'

He stood at the door uncertainly for a moment but she

would not look at him. He looked at the strips of bloodstained shirt on the floor where her mother had dropped them.

'I must pay you for that,' her mother said, noticing his look. He turned quickly, pulled the door shut without a word, and hurried home. Letting himself in, he went straight up to his room. He didn't want his mother to see him without his shirt, but mainly he needed to be by himself. He shut his door and threw himself on his bed, looking blankly up at the ceiling.

'Damn!' he said vehemently. 'Damn her!'

ADÈLE GERAS

A Long Ride on the Carousel

Last summer, I learned about love from Mr Fuller. It's not what you're thinking. That part of love, the physical part, is easy, compared with what Mr Fuller taught me. At first, I thought I'd write to Simon Bates and try to get on 'Our Tune', on Radio One, but I could never fit everything into the time: the feelings and the place and the people. So I'm writing it straight out, however long it takes.

I live in Seatown, which is a holiday resort. Seatown isn't its real name, and I'm not really Shirley, and all the other names that appear are made up by me. Apart from that, everything else is true.

The good thing about living in a seaside town is that you always know of someone who runs a boarding house or small hotel or B & B and who needs a hand during the season. Last July, I went to work the day school ended. Mrs Beecham's hotel was called The Abercrombie. There was another girl working there as well. Her name was Lorna. The Abercrombie was quite big: seven tables in the dining room and a little bar behind the desk and a TV lounge upstairs on the first floor. It was fairly clean. All the tablecloths were reasonably white and the lace curtains a lot less dingy than some I'd seen. Mrs Beecham kept the notices on the green baize board quite up-to-date. I only found one from the year before, drawing the attention of guests to the coronation of Seatown's Flower Queen.

The carpets throughout the hotel were a pattern of brown and orange whirlpools.

'I like a bit of colour' was one of the things Mrs Beecham was fond of saying, and there was a fair amount of it about in The Abercrombie, one way or another. Apart from the orange whirlpool carpets, there was rose trellis wallpaper in the bedrooms in a couple of dozen shades of mauve and purple and pink. The bathrooms had unnaturally blue shower curtains the colour of swimming pool water. At suppertime (6.00 pm to 7.30 pm Monday to Friday, 6.30 pm to 8.00 pm Saturday and Sunday) we served a different coloured soup each night, ranging from a tomato which almost matched the carpet, through beige mushroom, yellowish chicken, pale green leek, and dark brown minestrone to the glorious emerald of pea and bacon.

Lorna and I had our work cut out. There's plenty to do in a hotel, I can promise you. Beds to be made and covered up with candlewick bedspreads (fluffy yellow), loo rolls to check, tables to be cleared from breakfast and made up again with knives and forks etc ready for supper, cans of soup to be opened, the bar to be wiped down, the china ladies in crinoline dresses on the mantelpiece of the TV lounge to be dusted – it was never-ending. We hardly had a spare minute during the day and by the time evening came, we were generally too exhausted to do more than collapse on one of the shiny plastic seats of the Western Grill 'n' Griddle, across the road from The Abercrombie.

I didn't mind any of it. I loved it. I was happy, walking about on Cloud 9. The reason for this was Adam. Adam was my boyfriend. He was the first proper boyfriend I'd ever had, and nothing Mrs Beecham could throw at me could take the shine off my romance. And it *was* romantic, the way I'd met him. All my friends thought it was, and Lorna thought so too, when I told her. It happened like this.

Seatown's main promenade, which stretches from the fairground at one end to the leisure complex at the other, is just one long line of hotels and shops selling plastic shoes, sticks of rock, horrible T-shirts and animals made of shells. Also mugs with 'A gift from Seatown' printed on them. Every now and then there's an amusement arcade or a shooting gallery or a bingo place and dotted all along the prom, there are kiosks selling candy floss and soggy, grey burgers and limp sausages in stale buns. I try and keep away from it most of the time, but this day, the day I met Adam, I was walking along it for some reason. Every time I *did* go along the prom, I always used to stop and look at two things. I couldn't help it.

They fascinated me in the way that a chamber of horrors fascinates some people. They don't want to look, they *have* to look. What drew me, every time, was two life-size moving dummies in glass cases: Grandma Clampitt and the Laughing Clown. With the Laughing Clown (orange nylon hair, purple and white striped suit, huge lips the colour of blood in a chalk-white face) you had to put 10p in a slot, and then he would move, rock backwards and forwards and from side to side, while the rattle and grind of metal laughter filled the air. Children seemed to love it. Coin after coin would fall into the slot. I never put any money in, although perhaps I should have done. If the Laughing Clown was menacing when he moved, he was positively evil when he didn't. I had the feeling, even when there was no one about to put a 10p in, that he was just about to start moving as I passed his glass case. Crazy, right? Grandma Clampitt was even worse. She was an old lady in a long red and white gingham dress, sitting on a rocking chair with a rifle held across her knees. She had white hair in a bun and ice-coloured eyes. She was in a case just outside a shooting gallery and with her you didn't even need 10p. She would shudder into movement all by herself, worked by some kind of remote control. What she did was try and entice you in to have a go yourself with the guns and the targets.

'Come on, y'all,' she'd say in a voice like old razor-blades. 'It sho' is a whole lotta fun. Step right up, folks!' Then her chair would start rocking and rocking and the ice-coloured eyes would glitter as they caught the light of the neon sign above the glass case.

Anyway, one day I was looking at Grandma Clampitt and this yobbo starts on me. You know: hello darling, come and have a go with me then I'll buy you a Coke, any more at home like you . . . you know the kind of thing. He was horrible. I didn't even need to look at him to see he was horrible, and I turned as quickly as I could and tried to walk away, and then he put his hand on my arm, and tried to pull me back towards him. I nearly died. I couldn't think what to do. I wanted to scream and kick him and run away, but there's always another part of you that says: don't make a fuss, don't shout, don't draw attention to yourself. I couldn't move. I was paralysed. In the end I pulled my arm away and he pulled it back, exactly as if I were a rag-doll. Then I heard someone say: 'Doesn't look like she wants to go with you, does it, mate?' and like magic the horrible greasy hand left my arm. I turned and saw Adam. I could understand why the creep had disappeared. Adam was well over six feet tall and dressed in black from head to toe. He looked to me like a kind of angelic deliverer. I burst into tears.

'Hey?' he said. 'What's all this then? Haven't I just rescued you?'

'That's what I'm crying about,' I said. 'It's pathetic, needing to be rescued. I should be able to look after myself. I bet you think I'm a prize divvy.'

'No, I don't. I just think you're not used to things like that happening . . . or to nerds like him. If I hadn't come along, you'd have kicked him in the end.'

'I didn't want to make a fuss, though.'

'That's stupid. Promise me you won't care about that in future. That's really stupid.'

'O.K,' I said. 'I promise.'

'You look as if you could do with a coffee, or something,' he said. 'My name's Adam. What's yours?'

'Shirley.'

We went round the corner and had a coffee in the Western Grill 'n' Griddle – yes, the very same . . . the one opposite. The Abercrombie Hotel.

After that night, when I was so soppily and romantically rescued by my knight in black denim from the clutches of the dastardly villain on the prom, I saw Adam almost every day. One thing, as they say, led to another and in forty-eight hours I was in love. I thought about him every single minute. When I was with him, I couldn't let go his hand, couldn't tear my eyes away from him. I dreamed about him, went over our conversations again and again, felt myself flying into a million separate shining pieces every time he kissed me – I don't have to tell you. You know the sort of thing I mean. It's embarrassing to go into it in too much detail. The night Adam rescued me was May 13th. I started working at Mrs Beecham's on July 24th: six weeks or so of Paradise.

I saw less of Adam once I started work. He had a summer job too. We discussed it, and we both agreed that it would be good to have the extra money. Perhaps, we said, if we colleted enough between us, we could go on holiday together next year, somewhere far away from the flabby hot dogs and the smell of yesterday's fried onions.

Then one day about the middle of August, Mr Fuller arrived at The Abercrombie. I noticed him straight away, the very first time he came down to breakfast, because he was so different from the usual guest. I find it hard to tell people's ages, but he looked to me about seventy. He had white hair, and a longish face which seemed to have grooves cut into it. He wore a grey, three-piece suit, as though he weren't on holiday at all, but off to work in a bank or an office somewhere. As if that weren't strange enough, he always carried a plastic shopping bag around with him, whenever I saw him. The other thing that was remarkable about Mr Fuller was that he realised you were a person. Most visitors acted as though Lorna and I were invisible. Well, in my case, maybe that's just possible. I'm not exactly startling, but Lorna with her mane of red curls and her turquoise eyes – you'd have to be blind not to see her. Still, an absent 'Ta very much' was all we ever got from most people, with never so much as a glance in our direction. Mr Fuller spoke to us and took an interest in our answers.

'I'm sure I'm right in thinking,' he said to me one day, 'that this is just a holiday job.'

'Oh, yes,' I said. 'I'm going to be a TV cameraman. I mean camerawoman.'

'Nowadays,' he said, smiling at me, 'you're supposed to say 'cameraperson'.'

I liked him. I liked the way he took me seriously and joked with me at the same time. He even took the trouble to ask me what my name was. For the first three days of his stay, he vanished after breakfast, and only returned at suppertime to eat his colourful soup. I wondered, as I tidied his room, where he went and what he did, holding his plastic bag. All his personal stuff must have been in there, because his clothes and toilet things were all there was in his room. There was nothing that told you anything about him. His belongings could have been anyone's.

Lorna and I had different afternoons off. Mine was Wednesday, hers was Thursday. On this particular Wednesday, I had arranged to meet Adam at the fairground. He liked all those things: the Waltzer, the Roller Coaster, and especially the Carousel, with all the golden horses going round and round and up and down to the jangly music that was like no other music in the world. Just before I was about to set out to meet him, he rang me. He couldn't make it. There was a panic on at his hotel . . . never mind. I went to the fairground by myself in a foggy, nostalgic mood. It was a lovely day, one of the few sunny days of last summer. I wandered around, happily enough and eventually I ended up where I always ended up: beside the painted horses. I was looking at them going round and round and then I saw him: Mr Fuller was riding the Carousel in his three-piece grey suit and hugging his plastic shopping bag. Round and round he went, with the laughter and shrieks of the children on the other horses flying in the air around him. He stared straight in front of him, not seeing anything, not seeing me. I didn't want him to see me. I felt as though I'd caught him doing something embarrassing, something shameful. As the Carousel slowed down, I walked away. When I turned back to look, he was paying the man for another ride. He hadn't even got off his horse.

That evening, even though it was my day off, I'd agreed to help behind the bar. Mr Fuller was sitting alone at one of the little tables with a bowl of peanuts in front of him. He'd arranged a few of them in a circle, pushing them carefully with the tip of one finger till they were where he wanted them to be. I don't know what got into me then, why I said what I did. I went over, and before I could stop myself, the words came out:

'I saw you today, you know. Going round on the Carousel.'

He smiled. 'Good evening, Shirley. Why don't you sit down for a moment?'

I sat down on a small stool covered in crimson plush. I thought he wasn't going to say any more about it, but he did.

'Yes, the Carousel. I've always liked it. I go there every

afternoon. We came to Seatown on our honeymoon, my wife and I. Of course, that was a long time ago. Everything was different then. Quite different.'

I didn't stop to think. I should have. I mean, I could see how old Mr Fuller was . . . the possibility should have occurred to me. I said:

'Why have you come on your holiday all by yourself, then?'

'Because my wife is dead,' he answered and if I could have disappeared into one of the orange whirlpools on the carpet, I would have done, that very minute.

'I'm sorry,' I muttered, 'I should have thought. I *am* sorry, honestly.'

Mr Fuller smiled. 'It's perfectly all right. She is better, far better, being dead. She is at peace. I know, you see, because I killed her.'

I think I must have turned white or red or both, because he went on:

'There's no need to be alarmed. I am not, in the usual sense, a murderer. We made the plan together. We are old. She was dying. She couldn't bear the pain, and I couldn't bear to see her suffering. I could not watch the disease unfolding new shoots in her body every day.' He took two peanuts from the dish and placed them right in the centre of the circle made by the other peanuts. Then he looked up at me. I noticed for the first time (because I never look at old people, not properly) how blue his eyes were, how young-looking, how bright. He looked straight at me and said:

'I loved her very much, you see.'

'Yes,' I said lamely.

'On our honeymoon,' Mr Fuller continued, 'we used to ride the Carousel. "Do you love me?" she'd ask. And I'd say: "As long as the music goes round." People say the daftest things on their honeymoons . . . "As long as the music goes round" . . . and round and round we'd go.' He ate a peanut. 'Of course, it was all much cheaper then, going on the rides.'

I nodded. Mr Fuller took a sip of his beer. 'She said it to me again, that last night. "Do you love me?" she said. And I said: "As long as the music goes round." That's what I said to her, and I meant it. "Then let me go to sleep," she said, "and finish with all this hurting." So I did. I let her go to sleep. I dressed her in her best nightie and gave her drinking chocolate. I crushed all her sleeping pills into it and an extra spoon of sugar so that it shouldn't be too bitter for her.' He looked up at me and then saw that I was crying.

'I'm sorry,' he said. 'I shouldn't have said anything. I've gone and upset you now. Don't be sad. I'm not sad. We had over fifty years together. A long ride on the carousel. She's not in pain any more. I like to think of her like that: not hurting.' He finished his drink and stood up.

'Cheer up, Shirley. It'll all seem different tomorrow.' I smiled weakly as he left the room, carrying his shopping bag.

The next day when I arrived at The Abercrombie, there was a police car outside, which pulled away and vanished round the corner in a screech of rubber as I opened the door. I found Mrs Beecham in the kitchen, in a tizzy. It was hard to piece together what she was saying because it was all coming out in such a jumble, but I got the message soon enough. Mr Fuller was dead. The police had found him on a beach near the leisure complex, with his shopping bag beside him. There was a thermos flask, too. The police were analysing the contents. There was a note explaining that he had decided to end his own life, and another to Mrs Beecham with money in it for his bill and an apology for any upset.

'. . . and I must say,' said Mrs Beecham, 'it was considerate of him not to die in the hotel. Word does get round about that kind of thing, you know. It wouldn't be good for business, no indeed. Shirley, will you come with me and pack his belongings? The police will be calling for them later.'

I followed her upstairs. I thought: these shirts, this paisley scarf, this toothbrush, they aren't Mr Fuller. He's with his wife, I said to myself, comforting myself like a child. I didn't believe it in my heart of hearts, but I wanted to. I closed my eyes and forced a picture into my head of Mr Fuller and a pretty lady with white hair sitting together in a small room, on either side of a fireplace . . . of Mr Fuller and his bride like Adam and me, going round and round on the golden fairground horses. These pictures kept dissolving into tears. I stripped the bed and rolled the sheets and pillowslips into a bundle for the wash.

Over the next few weeks, I thought about Mr Fuller sometimes, but less and less each day, until by about the beginning of September, he had disappeared almost completely from my thoughts.

Then, one Thursday, Mrs Beecham asked me would I mind giving a hand in the bar that evening, after supper. I could have an hour or so off in the afternoon instead, even though it wasn't strictly my day off, but Lorna's. Yes, I said, and went off along the prom. There's no easy way of saying what happened next. I caught sight of Lorna's red hair a little way ahead of me, so I ran to catch up with her. I stopped almost immediately. Adam was with her, next to her, and just so that there should be nothing left unclear or shadowy, his arm was around her waist and she was leaning into his body as though she intended to grow into him. Not a thing you've heard or read or seen prepares you for what it feels like. Every single thing about the world and you in it feels wrong, feels bad. Every surface of your body is raw. I'm not proud of what I did after that. I followed them without them seeing me. I watched them walk into the Fairground. I saw them squeezed together into a round blue metal container on the Waltzer, but I turned away when he kissed her because I couldn't bear it. I don't know how I found my way back to The Abercrombie, but I did. I walked through the rest of the evening like a zombie, holding the pain somewhere right at the centre of me, where no one else could see it. I was suppoed to meet Adam in the Western Grill 'n' Griddle after work. All evening I'd been thinking: 'I won't go. I'll run away. I never want to see him again . . .' but by the time work finished, I'd changed my mind.

He was there when I arrived. He waved at me.

'Hi . . . I've got a Coke for you,' he said. I waved back.

'How's it been, then?' he said.

'Awful.'

'Why? What's the matter?'

I sat down and took a sip of my Coke and looked at him.

'I saw you and Lorna today. On the promenade. At the fairground. I don't think we should go out together anymore.'

Then he started with the talk, the chat, the words . . . hundreds of them, each one oilier and more untrue than the last . . . all the stuff you've ever heard about . . . Lorna didn't mean anything, just a silly flirtation, it was her fault anyway, she wouldn't leave him alone, won't happen again, you're the one for me . . . round and round the words went in my head, and every so often Grandma Clampitt joined in from round the corner, adding the steel echoes of her voice to Adam's. I listened for ages, but then I decided, all of a sudden, that I'd had enough. I finished the rest of my Coke and stood up.

'I'm going now,' I said. 'I've learned what real love is now, so all your stuff won't do any more. The trouble with you is, you think you love me, but you don't. Not really. Not enough. Not enough for me.' I turned and started to walk away from the table.

'How much *is* enough for you, then?' he shouted after me. 'What the hell do you want? Tell me that . . . go on, tell me. I'm waiting to hear.'

I called out to him over my shoulder as I stepped into the darkness.

'A longer ride on the Carousel,' I shouted and thought that somewhere, far away, I could hear the laughter of the Laughing Clown.

Clara's Day

When Clara Tilling was 15½ she took off all her clothes one morning in school assembly. She walked naked through the lines of girls, past the headmistress and the other staff, and out into the entrance lobby. She had left off her bra and pants already, so all she had to do was unbutton her blouse, remove it and drop it to the floor, and then undo the zipper of her skirt and let that fall. She slipped her feet out of her shoes at the same time and so walked barefoot as well as naked. It all happened very quickly. One or two girls giggled and a sort of rustling noise ran through the assembly hall, like a sudden wind among trees. The Head hesitated for a moment – she was reading out the tennis team list – and then went on again, firmly. Clara opened the big glass doors and let herself out.

The entrance lobby was empty. The floor was highly polished and she could see her own reflection, a fore-shortened pink blur. There was a big bright modern painting on one wall and several comfortable chairs for waiting parents, arranged round an enormous rubber plant and ashtrays on chrome stalks. Clara had sat there herself once, with her mother, waiting for an interview with the Head.

She walked along the corridor to her classroom, which was also quite empty, with thick gold bars of sunlight falling on the desks and a peaceful feeling, as though no one had been here for a long time nor ever would come. Clara opened the cupboard in the corner, took out one of the science overalls and put it on, and then sat down at her desk. After about a minute Mrs Mayhew came in carrying her clothes and her shoes. She said, 'I should put these on now, Clara,' and stood beside her while she did so. 'Would you like to go home?' she asked, and when Clara said that she wouldn't, thank you, Mrs Mayhew went on briskly, 'Right you are, then, Clara. You'd better get on with some homework, then, till the first period.'

All morning people kept coming up to her to say, 'Well done!' or just to pat her on the back. She was a celebrity right up till dinner time but after that it tailed off a bit. Half-way through the morning one of the prefects came in and told her the Head wanted to see her straight after school.

The Head's study was more like a sitting room, except for the big paper-strewn desk that she sat behind. She was busy writing when Clara came in: she just looked up to say, 'Hello, Clara. Sit down. Do you mind if I just finish these reports off? I won't be a minute.' She went on writing and Clara sat and looked at a photo of the Head's husband, who had square sensible-looking glasses, and her three boys who were all the same but different sizes. The Head slapped the pile of reports together and pushed her chair back. 'There . . . Well now . . . So what was all that about, this morning?'

'I don't know,' said Clara.

The Head looked at her, thoughtfully, and Clara looked back. Just before the silence became really embarrassing the Head said, 'I daresay you don't. Were you trying to attract attention?'

Clara considered. 'Well, I would, wouldn't I? Doing a thing like that. I mean – you'd be bound to.'

The Head nodded. 'Quite. Silly question.'

'Oh, no,' said Clara hastily. 'I meant you'd be bound to attract attention. Not be bound to be trying to.'

The Head asked, 'How do you feel about it now?'

Clara tried to examine her feelings, which slithered away like fish. In the end she said, 'I don't really feel anything,' which was, in a way, truthful.

The Head nodded again. 'Everything all right at home?'

'Oh, fine.' Clara assured her. 'Absolutely fine.'

'Good,' said the Head. 'Of course . . . I was just thinking, there are quite a lot of people in 4B with separated parents, aren't there? Bryony and Susie Tallance and Rachel.'

'And Midge,' said Clara. 'And Lucy Potter.'

'Yes. Five. Six, with you.'

'Twenty-five per cent,' said Clara. 'Just about.'

'Quite. As a matter of fact that's the national average, did you know? One marriage in four.'

'No, I didn't actually,' said Clara.

'Well, it is, I'm afraid. Anyway . . .'

'You're not fussing about GCSEs, are you?'

'Not really,' said Clara. 'I mean, I don't like exams, but I don't mind as much as some people.

'Your mocks were fine,' said the Head. 'Science could have been a bit better. But there shouldn't be any great problems there. So . . . Are you still going around with Liz Raymond?'

'Mostly,' said Clara. 'And Stephanie.'

'I want people to come and talk to me if there's anything they're worried about,' said the Head. 'Even things that may seem silly. You know. It doesn't have to be large obvious things. Exams and stuff. Anything.'

'Yes,' said Clara.

The phone rang. The Head picked it up and said no, she hadn't, and yes, she'd be along as soon as she could and tell them to wait. She put the receiver down and said, 'It wasn't like you, Clara, was it? I mean – there are a few people one wouldn't be *all* that surprised, if they suddenly did something idiotic or unexpected. But you aren't really like that, are you?'

Clara agreed that she wasn't, really.

'I'll be writing a note to your mother. And if you have an urge to do something like that again come and have a talk to me first, right?' The Head smiled and Clara smiled back. That was all, evidently. Clara got up and left. As she was closing the door she saw the Head looking after her, not smiling now, her expression rather bleak.

Most of the school had gone home but all those in Clara's class who had boyfriends at St. Benet's, which was practically everyone, were hanging around the bus station deliberately not catching buses because St Benet's came out half an hour later. Clara hung around for a bit too, just to be sociable, and then got on her bus. She sat on the top deck by herself and looked down onto the pavements. It was very hot; everyone young had bare legs, road menders were stripped to the waist, everywhere there was flesh – brown backs and white knees and glimpses of the hair under people's arms and the clefts between breasts and buttocks. In the park, the grass was strewn with sunbathers; there were girls in bikinis sprawled like starfish, face down with a rag of material between their legs and the strings of the top half undone. Clara, with no bra or pants on, could feel warm air washing around between her skin and her clothes. Coming down the stairs as the bus approached her stop, she had to hold down her skirt in case it blew up.

Her mother was already home. She worked part-time as a dentist's receptionist and had what were called flexible hours, which meant more or less that she worked when it suited her. Afternoons, nowadays, often didn't suit because Stan, her friend, who was an actor, was only free in the afternoons. Stan wasn't there today though. Clara came into the kitchen where her mother was drinking tea and looking at a magazine. 'Hi!' she said. 'Any news?' which was what she said most days. Clara said that there was no news and her mother went on reading. Presently she yawned, pushed the magazine over to Clara and went upstairs to have a bath. Clara had another cup of tea and leafed through the magazine and then began to do her homework.

The Head's letter came a couple of days later. Clara heard the post flop onto the doormat and when she looked over the bannister she knew at once what the typed envelope must be. At the same moment Stan, who had stayed the night, came out of her mother's room on his way to the bathroom. He wore underpants and had a towel slung round his neck like a football scarf, and was humming to himself. When he saw her he said, 'Wotcha! How's tricks, then?' and Clara pulled her dressing gown more closely round her and said, 'Fine thanks.'

'That's the stuff,' said Stan vaguely. 'Hey – I got a couple of tickets for the show. Bring a friend, OK?' He was a stocky muscular man with a lot of black hair on his chest. The smell of him, across the landing, was powerful – a huge inescapable wave of man smell: sweat and aftershave and something you could not put your finger on. Clara always knew when he was in the house before she opened the sitting room door because whiffs of him gusted about the place. She said, 'Thanks very much. That would be super,' and edged into her room.

When she came down they were both having breakfast.

Her mother was just opening the post. She said, 'Coffee on the stove, lovey. Oh goody – my tax rebate's come.' She opened the Head's letter and began to read. First she stared at it with a puzzled look and then she began to laugh. She clapped her hand over her mouth, spluttering. 'I don't believe it!' she cried. 'Clara, I simply do not believe it! Stan just listen to this . . . isn't she the most incredible girl! Guess what she did! She took off all her clothes in school assembly and walked out starkers!' She handed the letter to Stan and went on laughing.

Stan read the letter. Grinning hugely, he looked up at Clara. 'She'll have done it for a dare, I bet. Good on yer, Clara. Terrific! God, I wish I'd been there!' He patted Clara's arm and Clara froze. She went completely rigid, as though she had turned to cement, and when eventually she moved a leg it seemed as though it should make a cracking noise.

Her mother had stopped laughing and was talking again. '. . . the last thing anyone would have expected of you, lovey. You've always been such a prude. Ever since you were a toddler. Talk about modest! Honestly, Stan, she was hilarious, as a little kid – I can see her now, sitting on the beach at Camber clutching a towel round her in case anyone got a glimpse of her bum when she was changing. Aged 10. And when her bust grew she used to sit hunched over like a spoon so no one would notice it. And if she had to strip off for the doctor you'd have thought that he'd been about to rape her, from her expression. Even now I can't get her out of that Victorian one-piece school regulation bathing costume – and it's not as though she's not got a good shape.' 'Smashing!' said Stan, slurping his coffee.

'. . . spot of puppy fat still but that's going, good hips, my legs if I may say so. Which is what makes this such an absolute scream. Honestly, sweetie, I wouldn't have thought you had it in you. I mean, I've not been allowed to see her in the buff myself since she was 12. Honestly, I've wondered once or twice if there was something wrong with the girl.' Her mother beamed across the breakfast table. 'Anyway, old Mrs Whatsit doesn't seem to be making a fuss. She just thinks I ought to know. More coffee, anyone? God, look at the time! And I said

I'd be in early today . . . I'm off. Leave the breakfast things, lovey – we'll do them later. Coming Stan?'

Clara went on sitting at the table. She ate a piece of toast and drank her coffee. Her mother and Stan bustled about collecting her purse and his jacket and banged out of the house, shouting goodbye. The front gate clicked, the car door slammed, and then Clara began to cry, the tears dripping from her chin onto her folded arms and her face screwed up like a small child's.

Follow On

Whose Hair is it Anyway?

Before Reading

● What was the worst trouble you got into as a child? Describe the incident in detail. What finally happened?

During Reading

● Pause after the first paragraph. What kind of person is telling the story?

After Reading

● Think of five words which describe the person telling the story. Compare your choice of words with a friend's.

● Why do you think Rukshana became interested in hairdressing in the first place?

● Think back to your own childhood. What different crazes did you go through? Which lasted the longest and why?

The Salmon Cariad

Before Reading

● The story has an odd title. Any guesses what it will be about?

● People enjoy telling and hearing stories. Make a list of the stories you have either told or listened to during the past twenty-four hours. Remember to include jokes, soap operas, and songs.

During Reading

● Pause after the first paragraph. Do you think this is a true story? How can you tell? What clues are there?

After Reading

● How does the writer make the story sound as if it is being spoken aloud? Write down any words and phrases which sound like spoken rather than written English.

● Look back at the final sentence. Why do you think the storyteller finishes the story like this?

● Write your own legend based on the mysterious salmon. Read the first paragraph again and use this as the start of your story. But continue it in your own way. What happens this time when the salmon bites the fly . . .?

Eddy's Great Climb

Before Reading

● Why do some people dislike school? Whose fault is it? What could schools do to improve the situation?

● Here are some different reasons why pupils might enjoy school. Put them in order of most important down to least important.
– the teachers
– the equipment
– the uniform
– the subjects on offer
– strong discipline
– freedom for pupils

During Reading

● Pause after the third paragraph. What kind of person do you think Eddy is?

After Reading

● Use this chart to show Eddy's feelings for the items on the list on page 126:

Negative	Bored	Contented	Positive	Enthusiastic

School	Canoeing
Mrs Williams	John Page
Other teachers	Outdoor Centre
Computers	Climbing
Pauline Wood	Reading
Beer	

Discuss your answers with those of a friend.

● Imagine you are Eddy Wilson or Pauline Wood. Write a description of one of your days at the Joe Brown Outdoor Centre.

● What has been the most important event in your life so far? How did it change your attitudes?

The Wrestling Princess

Before Reading

● Think back to some of the fairy tales you remember. Make a list to show the typical qualities of a fairy tale prince and a fairy tale princess. How are they different?

● What are the 'ingredients' of a fairy tale? What kind of characters do they contain, what kind of stories, what kind of language? Discuss the ingredients with a partner.

During reading

● Pause after reading the first paragraph. In what ways does this story feel like a typical fairy tale? How does it seem different?

● Choose one sentence from the story which best describes the character of the Princess.

After Reading

● Does the story end in the way you might have guessed? How did you think it would end? What clues were there to hint at the ending of the story?

● Write down five words to describe the character of the King. Does he treat his daughter differently from other people at court? Explain how.

● Think of a fairy tale you know (for example, *Sleeping Beauty* or *Goldilocks*). Rewrite the story for a five-year-old reader making the characters behave in a way that we would not expect, giving them unusual personalities. Start your story with the words 'Once upon a time . . .'

The Secret Diary of Father Christmas Aged 57⅖⁷

Before Reading

● Think back to the days when you believed in Father Christmas. Choose three of these words and phrases which best describes your view of him:

cuddly	kind to reindeer
friendly	greedy
generous	hard working
old	well-organised
miserable	cheerful

Compare your three choices with those of a friend.

● When you were a young child what special preparations did you make for Santa's arrival?

After Reading

● Read each of the sentences below. For each one decide whether you think it is:
TRUE (T)
FALSE (F)
NOT ENOUGH EVIDENCE TO SAY (NEE)

Father Christmas has been asleep for eleven months.
Santa likes cold weather.
It took Santa 5½ hours to try out all the reindeer.
The temperature had fallen below −32°C during the year.
Santa killed two hundred reindeer.
Santa writes in his diary every day.
Santa gives everybody presents.
The first presents were delivered in America.
Santa delivered the last of his presents in Germany.
Santa really enjoys Christmas.
Rudolph has a baby called Rudy.
The story is very funny.

● Look back at the diary entry for 3rd December. Write *Rudolph's* diary for that day. Do not forget to mention:
– falling asleep in Santa's kitchen
– complaining about the cold in the shed
– eating cornflakes
– packing into the shed to keep warm.

You might start off like this:

3rd December

What a day! It started off, as usual, with miserable old Santa Claus getting us all to see how quickly we could run and how high we could jump. What a performance! First . . .

Beautiful Tara

Before Reading

● What does the term UFO mean? Which of these statements about UFOs do you agree with?
1 We cannot prove that UFOs exist, but we also cannot prove that they do not exist.
2 It is more likely that UFOs do not exist than that they do.
3 The kind of people who believe in UFOs are the kind of people who believe in ghosts.
4 UFOs are only seen by people who want to see them.

● If an alien did come to Earth from space what do you think it might look like? (You might do an illustration.)

During Reading

● After reading the first page of the story, what clues are there that something unusual is about to happen? What do you guess the Corn Circles are?

After Reading

● What was the first sign that Tara was dangerous?

● What effect does Tara's visit have on the person telling the story?

● How does his attitude towards her change during the story?

● Think up your own story about an unusual visitor who seems at first to be normal. Then describe how you find out that he or she has dangerous qualities.

Master of the Universe

Before reading

● Look at the title of this story. What do you think it will be about? Who will the characters be? Where and when will the story be set?

● Look at this list of relationships:
Parents
Grandparents
Sister/brother
Aunt/uncle
Best friend
Teacher

Now look at this list of situations. Draw a table to show which of these people you would turn to in each situation. You are:
– feeling unwell
– in serious trouble
– worried about school
– not getting on with a friend
– short of money to go out
– angry with a parent.

Think of other situations. Who do you turn to most? In what kind of situations is your friend most important? When is your family more important?

During Reading

● Look at the third section of the story (from 'Martin lay on his bed . . .' on page 42 to 'He waited' on page 44. Which is the most important sentence? Why?

● Pause before reading the final section on page 47. What will happen?

After reading

● Think back to what you predicted the story would be about based on the title. Were you right? Why do you think the story was called *Master of the Universe*? Think of a different title.

● The story is told in quite a confusing way. Using no more than five sentences, tell the story in a more direct way.

● Which of these statements best describes Martin (a) at the beginning of the story, (b) at the end of the story?:
Martin is angry.
Martin is selfish.
Martin is cheerful.
Martin is sad.
Martin is confused.
Martin is cruel.
Martin wants to be left alone.

Martin does not really want to be left alone.
Martin cares a lot about his guinea pigs.

● Imagine you are Martin's mother. Describe the way Martin has changed during the past few months. What *was* he like? How has he changed? How do you feel about this?

The Shrimp

Before Reading

● Discuss this issue in small groups: Why do people bully? Does bullying always have to involve physical violence or are there other forms of bullying too?

After Reading

● Only one of these summaries of the story is true. Say which one and describe what is wrong with the other four.
1 Two bullies drown a dog belonging to a small boy.
2 A boy drowns trying to rescue a dog.
3 Despite being bullied by two boys, an 11 year old boy rescues his dog.
4 Two bullies rescue a dog belonging to an 11 year old boy.
5 A dog is rescued by two bullies who then keep it.

● Either:
Think of a time when you were bullied. Why did it happen? What form of bullying was it? What finally ended it? How do you feel about it now?
Or:
Think of a time when you bullied someone else. Why? What emotions did you feel as a bully? What finally happened? How do you feel about the incident now?

Just Testing

Before Reading

● Are you a loner or do you usually go round with a group of friends? What do you think leads people to join gangs? Are people who prefer to be on their own unhappy?

● Which of the following ideas is the most important to you? Put them in order of most important to least important.

money	health
happiness	success at school
friendship	being liked
being a leader	being an individual

After Reading

- Think of two reasons why Rob wants to join Pete and Tom's gang.

- How has Rob's view of the gang changed by the end of the story?

- What do you think the author means when he says that Rob went home 'burning' (page 59)?

- Look at the part of the story where Rob brings the pheasant to show the others. Imagine you are either Pete or Tom and describe the scene, showing how you felt as you watched Rob approaching.

They Flee from Me

Before Reading

- Why do you think some people keep pets? Which animals make the best pets? Why?

- Are there some animals which people keep as pets which you think are unsuitable? Why?

During Reading

- Pause after the first sentence. What do you predict will happen in the rest of the story?

- Pause after the policeman knocks on the door. What news do you think he has brought?

After Reading

- Working in pairs, read the story through again. One of you should make a list of the points which show Frank behaving kindly towards the dog, whilst the other lists the points when he behaves cruelly. Then compare the notes you have made. What do they show about Frank's attitude to his pet?

- How would you describe the policeman's attitude to Frank and his wife? Why does he think that they shouldn't be allowed to keep a dog? Do you agree with him?

- How would you treat a dog with similar problems?

- Read the last paragraph of the story again. How does Frank feel now that the dog has been returned home?

Keep Quite Still

Before Reading

● Discuss in groups of 3 or 4 the most frightening experience you have ever had. As a group, decide which one of these is the most frightening and share it with the rest of the class.

During Reading

● Pause after the third paragraph. What is surprising about the way the person on the airbed reacts to the sharp pain? How would you have reacted?

After Reading

● What is the first sign that something unusual is happening to the child on the airbed?

● Imagine you are the mother of the child. Describe your reactions when you are told what happened to him.

● Imagine you are one of the little people. Describe your journey from the child's fingers up into his nose. What obstacles did you have to overcome and which areas were the most dangerous?

Moving

Before Reading

● Have you ever moved house? What are your memories of the experience – enjoyable, exciting, messy, depressing . . .?

● Think back over the main events in your life. What was the most important thing to happen to you, something which has perhaps changed your life? Why was it so important?

During Reading

● Read to the end of the paragraph where the father comes in (it ends on page 70 with 'Mum could see the young woman'). What will happen next?

● Choose one word each to describe the behaviour of the mother, the father and the young woman.

After Reading

● Why is the family moving house again?

● How can you tell that the person telling the story is young? What clues are there?

● Think of a different title for the story.

● None of the characters says very much about his or her feelings. Choose either the mother, father or young woman and write down what they might be thinking when they are all in the room together.

Lucy and the Dolphins

Before Reading

● Make a list of six subjects you take at school. Using a scale of five (top) down to one (bottom), mark stars next to each subject. For example, if English is your best subject you might give it *****.
Which subjects came top? Why do you think this is? Is it because you are good at them, because of the teacher or simply because you enjoy them?

● Using the same scale put stars next to this list of eight personal qualities:

determination	helpfulness
honesty	concentration
patience	getting on with other people
reliability	taking advice

Now look back at the subject which you scored most highly in. Which of these personal qualities do you need most for that? Fill in the stars against the list for a friend: see how far your list is similar to the one she or he made.

During Reading

● Pause after the first paragraph. What kind of person do you think is writing this story?

After Reading

● Discuss these questions:
Why do you think Lucy is unhappy?
Why do you think Lucy decided to flip the coin?
What is surprising about the way Lucy's teachers react when Lucy stops being good?

● What are the arguments for and against keeping animals in zoos? Which animals should we leave in the wild? Do you think any animals gain from being kept in zoos?

● Do you think Lucy was right to release the dolphins? Be prepared to explain your answer.

You Never Know What You've Got Till It's Gone

Before Reading

● Have you ever felt like running away from home? What caused you to feel like this? What finally happened?

● What is the worst event that has happened in the area where you live? Do other people in your class agree with you?

After Reading

● Why do you think Annie lies to Rose about the way her brother had vanished?

● What happens next in the story? Read it through again and then continue it, showing what happens to Annie. Does she get into 'awful trouble' as Rose says?

The Gallows Haunting

Before Reading

● For discussion: Is there any evidence that ghosts exist? Have you ever seen a ghost yourself or do you know of someone who has? What is the most frightening ghost story you have heard, or seen in a film?

● What are the ingredients of a good ghost story? Put the items in this list in order of importance:

Powerful atmosphere	Story set in the past
Bloodthirstiness	Strong characters
Suspense	Plenty of description
Spooky setting	Horrific ghosts or monsters

During Reading

● Which sentence during the first two pages tells you that this is going to be a ghost story?

After Reading

● Which part of the story was the most frightening? Explain why.

● On a scale of 1 to 10 say how frightening you found the story. What would have made it more frightening? Discuss your ideas with a friend.

Dad, Can I Come Home?

Before Reading

● Think about life in the future. What new inventions do you think will be created during the next 20 years. Make a list of five ideas.

● This story is set in the future. Why do you think many people enjoy reading science fiction or watching sci-fi films and programmes? What is the attraction?

● Look again at the title of the story. What do you think it will be about?

During Reading

● Draw two columns. In one, write down the details in the story that show you it is set in the future. In the other, write down details which could take place in the present.

● Pause halfway through the story (at the paragraph ending '. . . and cried' on page 92). What will happen next?

After Reading

● What are Mr Walker's real reasons for not wanting Janice to stay?

● Why has Eve killed herself?

● Look back through the story. What clues were there that it was Eve, not Janice, who was disabled?

● In pairs, think about the advantages and disadvantages of setting the story in the future. How would it have been different if set in the present?

Otherworld

Before Reading

● Why do you think people keep pets? Which pets do you think are:
– the most useful?
– the most attractive?
– the most friendly?
– the most unsuitable?
Discuss your ideas with a friend.

● Some people say that pets reflect the character and looks of their owners. Choose five people in your class and imagine which pets would be most suitable for them. Use cartoons to bring your ideas to life.

During Reading

● Pause after the second paragraph. What do you find unusual about the story so far?

After Reading

● Which of these words best describes the cat's relationship with its owner?

aggressive   untrusting
loving   cruel
annoyed

● Imagine you are one of the following pets:
dog; rat; goldfish; hamster; bird; spider.

Describe an unexpected meeting with a human being. What are your first impressions? How does the human react? What happens? Give as much detail as you can.

Deeper and Deeper

Before Reading

● What is your idea of how to spend a perfect summer's day?

● Write a paragraph about a time when you were wrongly blamed for something you did not do.

During Reading

● As you read the story, look out for clues about the boy and girl's relationship. How long have they known each other?

● What different dangers are shown in the story?

After Reading

● Why do you think the writer does not tell us the names of the boy and girl?

● Why does the girl's mother react so suspiciously towards the boy?

● Why does this upset the boy so much?

● Imagine the boy and girl meet up next day. Write down the conversation that would take place between them.

A Long Ride on the Carousel

Before Reading

● Do you know what a carousel is? Which of these words best describes it?
a seesaw
a merry-go-round
a kind of bus
a type of toffee

● Think back over holidays you have enjoyed. Do you think that the kind of holiday you like changes as you get older? Explain how.

During Reading

● Pause at the end of the first paragraph. Use this list to describe the character telling the story:
male/female
under 12
12 to 16
over 16

How can you tell? What clues in the first paragraph helped you to reach your decision?

● How does the narrator change during the story?

After Reading

● Why does Mr Fuller kill himself? Why has he chosen Seatown to do this?

● Why did Mr Fuller kill his wife? Imagine that he has left a letter explaining why he did this. Write his letter.

● Put yourself in Shirley's position. How would you react if you had seen Adam with another girl? Why does Shirley delay telling Adam that she can see him? Was she right not to face up to him on the spot?

● What has Shirley learned by the end of the story?

Clara's Day

Before Reading

● Do you attend a mixed school or a single-sex school? What are the advantages and disadvantages of teaching girls altogether or boys altogether?

● Discuss in a small group the following questions:
How do people try to attract attention to themselves? How do
people dress or behave differently in order to be noticed? Does
'being fashionable' mean being an individual or being one of the
crowd?

During Reading

● Stop reading after the first paragraph. What do you think is going
to happen in the rest of the story?

After Reading

● What is surprising about the way the Headmistress reacts to what
Clara has done?

● How is the school Clara goes to different from yours? Make a list.

● Imagine you are Clara. Write about your feelings towards your
mum's friend, Stan. How did you feel when you first met him? What
do you like or dislike about him? How have your feelings for your
mother changed since Stan first arrived?

Reading Projects

● Choose your three favourite stories from this book and write an
introduction to them for someone who does not read very often.
Describe the stories briefly (without giving away the endings) and
say why you like them.

● What do you consider the most important ingredients of a good
short story? Make a list and explain your ideas. Which of the stories
in this book contains the most items on your list?

● Consider the title of this book. What would be a better title? What
would have been a better cover to attract people to read the book?

● Many of the characters in the stories are fiercely individual – they
do not simply 'follow the crowd'. Write a comparison of three such
characters using the title 'Individualists'.

Further Reading

The following list of reading suggestions should help you to explore your own interests and enthusiasms. All of the titles are available in paperback; many will be in your school library.

Humour

The Eighteenth Emergency, Betsy Byars, Puffin; *Boy* and *Going Solo*, Roald Dahl, Penguin; *Funnybones*, (Ed.) Trevor Millum, HarperCollins; *Confessions of a Teenage Baboon*, Paul Zindel, Lions.

Supernatural

The Woman in Black, Susan Hill, Longman; *Ghostly and Ghastly*, Barbara Ireson, Hamlyn; *The Whitby Witches*, Robin Jarvis, Simon and Schuster; *The Wind Eye*, Robert Westall, Penguin.

Science fiction/fantasy

Spellhorn, Berlie Doherty, Lions; *Grinny*, Nicholas Fisk, Penguin; *The Fifth Child*, Doris Lessing, Paladin; *Truckers*, Terry Pratchett, Corgi.

Relationships

Forever, Judy Blume, Puffin Plus; *The Friends*, Rosa Guy, Penguin; *Buddy* and *Buddy's Song*, Puffin Plus; *Of Mice and Men*, John Steinbeck, Heinemann.

Acknowledgements

The editors and publisher are grateful to the following for permission to reproduce the short stories in this collection:

'Whose Hair is it Anyway?' © Beverley Naidoo: reproduced by permission of Roger Hancock Limited; 'The Salmon Cariad' © Alan Garner: published by HarperCollins Publishers in *A Bag of Moonshine*; 'Eddy's Great Climb' and 'Lucy and the Dolphins' © Richard Bennett (with thanks to all the staff and students I have been associated with); 'The Wrestling Princess' © Judy Corbalis: first published by Scholastic Publications Limited in *The Wrestling Princess and Other Stories*; 'The Secret Diary of Father Christmas, Aged 57½' © Synte Peacock; 'Beautiful Tara' © Nicholas Fisk 1991: reproduced by permission of Laura Cecil; 'Master of the Universe' © Tim Crawley (Thank you, Victoria, for all your support and faith); 'The Shrimp' © David Harmer; 'Just Testing' and 'Otherworld' © Roy Samson; 'They Flee from Me' © Adrian Burke; 'Keep Quite Still' © Trevor Millum; 'Moving' and 'Deeper and Deeper' © Roger Burford-Mason; 'You Never Know What You've Got Till It's Gone' by Fay Weldon appears in print here for the first time and is reproduced by kind permission of the author and Sheil Land Associates, 43 Doughty Street, London WC1N 2LF to whom requests to reproduce the story should be made; 'The Gallows Haunting': an abridged version of a longer story by Susan Harr, who retired from teaching recently in order to travel and work abroad, and also to pursue an interest in writing; 'Dad, Can I Come Home?': first published in the short story collection *Not So Stupid!* by Malorie Blackman, published by Livewire Books For Teenagers, November 1990; 'A Long Ride on the Carousel' © Adèle Geras: published by HarperCollins Publishers in *Someday My Prince Won't Come* (Lions Teentracks); 'Clara's Day' © Penelope Lively: published by William Heinemann Ltd and Penguin Books Ltd in *Pack of Cards*.

Although every effort has been made to contact the copyright-holders, this has not proved to be possible in every case. We apologise for any inadvertent infringements of copyright.